BETWEEN SHADOWS

 **bitlit**

A **free** eBook edition is available
with the purchase of this print book.

- -

CLEARLY PRINT YOUR NAME ABOVE IN UPPER CASE

Instructions to claim your free eBook edition:
1. Download the BitLit app for Android or iOS
2. Write your name in **UPPER CASE** on the line
3. Use the BitLit app to submit a photo
4. Download your eBook to any device

www.coteaubooks.com

BETWEEN SHADOWS

KATHLEEN COOK WALDRON

Edited by Kathy Stinson
Cover by Tania Craan
Typeset by Susan Buck
Printed and bound in Canada

Library and Archives Canada Cataloguing in Publication

Waldron, Kathleen Cook, author
        Between shadows / Kathleen Cook Waldron.

Issued in print and electronic formats.
ISBN 978-1-55050-612-9 (pbk.).--ISBN 978-1-55050-613-6 (pdf).--
ISBN 978-1-55050-819-2 (epub).--ISBN 978-1-55050-820-8 (mobi)

        I. Title.

PS8595.A549B48 2015   jC813'.54   C2014-908230-4
                                            C2014-908231-2

Library of Congress Control Number 2014955928

2517 Victoria Avenue
Regina, Saskatchewan
Canada S4P 0T2
www.coteaubooks.com

10 9 8 7 6 5 4 3 2 1

Available in Canada from:
Publishers Group Canada
2440 Viking Way
Richmond, British Columbia
Canada V6V 1N2

Available in the US from:
Orca Book Publishers
www.orcabook.com
1-800-210-5277

Coteau Books gratefully acknowledges the financial support of its publishing program by: the Saskatchewan Arts Board, The Canada Council for the Arts, the Government of Canada through the Canada Book Fund, the City of Regina, and the Government of Saskatchewan through Creative Saskatchewan.

For Rosy and Levi

CHAPTER ONE

WHEN I WAS LITTLE, Gramps was like Santa Claus: a jolly old man who showed up once a year with presents. I never knew much about his life the rest of the year. But the summer I was nine, our family packed up our clunker and drove across the country to Gramps' cabin in the woods. That road trip and our time at the cabin were the happiest and the saddest days of my life.

That summer Gramps taught me to swim. He showed me how to paddle his red canoe and how to fish. Together we reeled in my first trout. I can still feel it zinging my line, pure muscle as silvery as water.

He showed me how to pick mushrooms that wouldn't poison me and how to pick berries so they wouldn't get smushed. Every morning I woke up with the same big, fat smile I fell asleep with.

Then the accident happened. Dad and I went home. Mom came with us – in a box. People say her spirit is in heaven, but who really knows? It's not like she sends texts or postcards.

Dad told Gramps not to come here, and for three years we didn't go there. Then last fall, when I turned twelve, me and Gramps made a plan. He'd fixed up his cabin and wanted to surprise me with its awesome new paint job. As soon as school let out for the summer, I would fly *by myself* to Vancouver. Aunt Laurel would meet me and put me on the bus to Gramps' cabin. We'd spend the whole summer together. Just me and Gramps. We spent hours talking about fishing and swimming and seeing wildlife and eating raspberries. We even talked about an overnight canoe trip, camping out under the stars...

Our plan was perfect until Gramps died in March.

"Ari, Ari! Leave the dishes," Dad calls from the couch. "Come here. I've been thinking."

"Uh oh. Thinking about what?" I wipe my hands and turn away from the sink. Dad mutes a beer commercial and unslouches himself. He puts down the latest piece of wood to fall victim to his knife. Carving, he calls it.

"Let's go to Pop's cabin, you and me, together," he says.

"But why? Why go without Gramps?"

"Aunt Laurel's going up there, and now that school's out I think we should too. We have to settle his estate, and who knows what she'll do if I don't keep an eye on her? Besides, a change of scenery might do us good."

My mouth drops open, but no words come out. The man hasn't cracked a smile in three years. Not since the accident. And now he's saying that trapping ourselves in the wilderness with Aunt Laurel at Gramps' empty cabin might cheer him up?

Seriously?

CHAPTER TWO

AUNT LAUREL HASN'T CROSSED MY PATH in years, except by phone, but I recognize her instantly. Who could forget her spiky hair, pink today, or the fairies dangling from her earlobes? She locks eyes first on Dad and then on me, scowling for all she's worth.

"Boy, do you two need haircuts!" she shouts over the bus station crowd.

Dad rolls his eyes. I get the hairy part – she's a hairdresser – but fairies?

Without asking about our trip or pausing long enough for us to speak, she pelts us with complaints about all the work she's had to do in the three weeks she's been here ahead of us: the clutter she's had to clear, the cleaning, and oh, the drudgery of it.

Dad loads our suitcases into her trunk. I try to blend in with a quiet group of normal people getting into a taxi. "Where are you headed?" the driver asks them with a friendly smile. Doors slam.

We get into Aunt Laurel's dinged-up jalopy and drive to a grocery store. "Aren't you coming in?" Dad asks.

I shake my head.

"Suit yourself." Aunt Laurel slams the door.

As soon as they're out of sight, I climb out of the backseat, stand up and stretch, breathing in the dusty parking lot air.

I lean against the car and watch people push shopping carts into and out of the store. Ordinary people buying ordinary stuff. My eyes feel heavy, so I climb back into the car and sprawl out on the backseat.

Next thing I know, we're lurching from stop sign to stop sign, leaving the town of Moose Valley behind us. We pick up speed, and I buckle my seat belt. Aunt Laurel zooms through straight aways then whacks us into our seat backs when she slams on the brakes for the curves. The pavement ends and we hit the gravel with a crunchy skid.

"Watch for logging trucks," she warns us as we reel from side to side.

Dad stares blankly ahead. I try not to throw up.

After an hour of bumps and turns, we stop at a steel gate plastered with "Keep Out" and "No Trespassing" signs. Aunt Laurel hands Dad the key.

"I don't remember Pop mentioning a gate," he says.

"He didn't," she replies. "After Father passed away in March, I hired someone to install it. An abandoned place is an open invitation to vandalism and theft. I'm sure I told you."

"Maybe you did."

"Anyway, the cost will come out of the estate. Here's the key. Be sure to lock the gate behind us."

Dad does as he's told, then walks behind the car rather than getting back in.

The long driveway cuts between a small meadow on the right and tall trees on the left, just like I remember it. Gramps' cabin comes into view in a sunny clearing beyond the trees.

"Holy granola!" I gasp. Each log is a different colour: shades of purple, blue, orange and yellow with a bright red door, all under a red tin roof. A rainbow house! Awesome!

"Weird, isn't it?" Aunt Laurel says. "When I first saw it I couldn't believe it either. Father told me he painted the place and had it re-roofed last fall, but I never asked for details. He must have used up a lot of leftover paint."

We stop beside the front porch and climb out of the car.

The weeds in front of the cabin have been driven over again and again. Tire tracks go every which way. The rest of the yard has grown wild. Tall grass and tangles of weeds have swallowed up Gramps' garden.

A hand on my shoulder makes me jump. "Look," Dad says, his eyes shiny with tears, "The swing."

I lean against him, scanning the garden for the swing where we posed for our last family photo, the four of us. Gramps called us a Martin sandwich, with him and Dad on the outside and me on Mom's lap filling up the middle.

The empty swing hovers over the weeds like a giant insect.

Aunt Laurel pops the trunk. "Enough gawking," she says. "Get your things and help me with these groceries."

Inside, the cabin is how I remember it. Walls of log-coloured logs. The entire downstairs is an open kitchen/living area except for two small rooms and an even smaller bathroom. Aunt Laurel has already claimed the larger room for herself, leaving the other for her brother.

I leave my bags of groceries on the kitchen table and haul my backpack up the sturdy ladder leading to the loft: my room, the one Gramps saved just for me. I drop my pack on the floor and flop on the bed, my bed. A real bed with a real quilt. I savor its bed-ness. Back in Toronto, Dad said a sleeping bag on the couch is like getting to camp out every night. Ha! I had to come to the wilderness to escape our small-as-a-tent apartment.

Sun pours in through the skylight. Gramps promised me

the sun, the moon and millions of stars. He never mentioned clouds racing by. I tuck my hands under my head. "Well, Gramps, here I am. Finally. But where are you?"

"Ari, get down here. We're not finished," Aunt Laurel calls sharply.

I toss my stuff into the small dresser and place our family photo on top.

"Ari!" Aunt Laurel calls again, louder, harsher.

More unloading. More organizing. Followed by salad duty while Dad sets the table and Aunt Laurel fries nut burgers and heats canned beans.

Our meatless meal includes a dinner-length Aunt Laurel complaint-a-thon.

"You simply can't imagine," she drones on, "the clutter I had to haul. Not to mention the washing and scrubbing and dusting and mousing and..."

"Mousing?" I ask, but she's already complaining about something else.

After dinner and washing up, Dad wanders over to the living room window and stands there, silent. Minutes pass before he says, "Police don't come about fish."

For a second I think I misheard him. And then I remember.

Three years ago in this very spot, I said something like, "Look, Gramps, a policeman's coming up the driveway. Did we catch too many fish?"

Dad and Gramps came over to the window with me, and Gramps said, "Police don't come about fish."

We stood at the window while the cop drove past the garden, so slowly he didn't stir up a speck of dust. The car stopped at the front porch. The cop walked up the steps.

Still, we stood at the window: father, son and son of son. A family about to change forever.

Aunt Laurel's voice breaks the spell. "Would you believe our only connection to the outside world is an old-fashioned phone? We have no cell service, and Father never got Internet. No television either. I thought about installing them, but since we won't be here long, I figured it was a waste of money. We'll just have to entertain ourselves."

And so we do. Aunt Laurel pulls out a magazine. Dad goes to work on his chunk of wood. I sit in Gramps' rocker, listening to my tunes and playing games I don't need the Internet for. Just like at home but without the television blaring in the background.

We sit for hours or maybe only minutes, a family still life. Dad puts down his carving and opens his guitar case. I slip away to the loft. Still life minus one.

In bed I listen to Dad strum the guitar he vowed to learn to play this summer. His strumming sets off Aunt Laurel's whining. No sirens or screeching tires interrupt their duet. And instead of headlights or streetlights, only starlight shines in my window.

CHAPTER THREE

"ARI, YOUR PORRIDGE is getting cold."

I open my eyes to bright sunshine, dress and obediently go down to my bowl of mush.

"I have just enough time to make you and your father decent before he and I leave for town."

"Town?" Dad says. "Again?"

"Decent?" I ask.

"One question at a time," Aunt Laurel says. "James, you and I meet with the lawyer today to go over the estate. I didn't make the appointment for yesterday because I figured you and Ari needed to settle in first. And to answer you, Ari, decent boils down to one word: haircuts. We'll do them outside so we don't mess up the house. Then you can start cleaning up the yard while your father and I are gone."

Hair and scissors fly. Aunt Laurel may not be the world's best hairdresser, but she sure is fast. Before the last hair settles in the grass, Dad and Aunt Laurel are in the car and she's yelling out the window, "You'll find work gloves in the garden shed."

Freshly trimmed and itchy, I slog through the weeds to a shed in the corner of the garden. I turn the latch gingerly, listening for the skittering of rats or bats. The door swings open. Nothing moves.

Inside, the shed is musty, covered with cobwebs and filled with well-cared-for tools, Gramps' tools. Some hang from nails, others dangle from hooks, several sit neatly on shelves. A full box of bright red plastic ribbon sits on one shelf. Was Gramps planning to wrap a lot of packages? Two fishing poles stand in a corner. A snow scoop and a shovel rest against the back wall.

I find a pair of nearly new work gloves and take the shovel outside, running my fingers along the smooth, wide grooves that Gramps' fingers wore into its wooden D-handle.

Where are those raspberries me and Gramps picked and ate by the handful? Those heavy clusters of deep red berries with tiny gold whiskers, warm with sunshine, juicy sweet and crunchy with seeds, so ripe they fell into my hand. All I've tasted lately are ice-cold berries nicked quickly from too-expensive boxes in the market.

If I clear some weeds, maybe I'll find some berries. I start hacking tall thistles with the shovel and pulling up smaller weeds with my hands. Some surrender easily. Others fight back. I hack and pull till my arms ache.

Still no berries, but I've had enough weeds. Time for a break.

I down a quick sandwich and grab my favourite baseball cap, the Colorado Rockies one Gramps gave me. He'd never been to Colorado, but he liked the logo, said it reminded him how rocky patches can also be beautiful. That's Gramps for you. I head out to start exploring the only way I can – on foot.

Once I'm over the gate, I turn right, away from town. That way, if Dad and Aunt Laurel return early, they won't ruin my adventure.

I break into a trot. My feet pound the gravel road, pumping city air out, sucking forest air in. My cap slips over my eyes. I push it back. Why'd Aunt Laurel have to chop off my hair?

Left, right, left, right.

Next time I'll bring my tunes.

Right, left, right, left.

Beads of sweat drip down my neck.

"Hey," a voice calls behind me. "You!"

Left, right, left.

"You, jogger boy, where are you going?"

Right, left.

"Are you deaf?" Louder this time. "I asked you where you're going."

Great. Even in the middle of nowhere, bullies find me. Head down, I focus on my feet.

Left, right – THWACK!

A purple mountain bike cuts in front of me and sends me sprawling.

"Is this what you runners call 'hitting the wall'?" says the girl on the bike now blocking my path. She's about my size, though she seemed bigger when she cut me off. "You must be new. Are you staying at the campground or visiting someone? Why haven't I seen you before?"

I pick myself up, brushing leaves and dirt off my clothes. Sunlight sparks from her wild hair, as if her head were on fire.

"Perfect, new and mute. Just my luck," she says, and as quickly as she appeared, she's gone.

A murder of crows caws by. Trees reach high above me, their shadows dark and quick. The road around me is empty. A girl on a bike is no big deal, but her unexpectedness reminds me of Gramps' encounters with foxes, bears, cougars and who knows what other wild creatures I'd rather not think about right now.

I turn back the way I came, head down, feet pounding faster, faster.

CHAPTER FOUR

"ALL THREE OF US NEED TO BE PRESENT for the reading of the will."

Meaning what? Neither Dad nor Aunt Laurel tries to explain. Maybe they don't know themselves. But after another quiet night and another rushed breakfast, we're on the road again.

Roller coasters have fewer bumps and curves than the road into town. Aunt Laurel's fairy earrings hug the curves like Grand Prix racers while her pink-streaked hair clings to her head like a helmet.

We park in front of a small office building on the main street. A shiny bronze sign on the door reads, "Sanders & Foster, Barristers."

I slide out of the car onto pudding legs, half expecting the car roof to bulge where my head jack-hammered it on the ride in. My seat belt may have kept me from ricocheting around the backseat, but nothing could stop the bouncing.

"At least the dust covers the rust," Dad says, running a finger along his door and leaving a blue streak in the brown dirt. Aunt Laurel glares at him. "It's true, Sis. Dust is almost as good as a new paint job. Cheaper too."

She grins in spite of herself. Lame as it was, Dad actually tried to make a joke. When was the last time that happened?

Aunt Laurel opens the building door and leads us up steep, narrow stairs. A mural of roly-poly women in colourful robes and scarves soars up the wall beside us. A decidedly not roly-poly woman in a pale business suit greets us at the front desk.

"Mr. Foster is expecting you," she says. "Follow me."

She ushers us through a heavy door with thick frosted glass, down a hallway to another door. She knocks and calls, "The Martins are here."

"Show them in, Mrs. Bradley," a voice booms from the other side. Mrs. Bradley shows us in then snaps the door shut, leaving us alone with Mr. Foster and a Mountie.

Names bounce back and forth like tennis balls. We're invited to sit on cushy black chairs.

"We're here today to read the last will and testament of Mr. Walter Martin, as fine a gentleman as I've ever known," Mr. Foster says. "Constable Nelson has agreed to serve as our official witness to guarantee that young Ari Martin has been clearly advised of his grandfather's wishes. Seeing as the constable has other responsibilities and we're all busy people, I'll be quick. Walter wanted me to read you this letter:

> *Dear Family,*
>
> *By the time you get this, I'll have moved on to other places. I suspect they're no better than what I've left behind, but I'm hoping they won't be worse. You likely think I'm an old hermit who chose life in the bush over being with you, but nothing could be further from the truth — you were with me every moment.*
>
> *Laurel and James, after the accident, I kept inviting you back to Canoe Lake for a reason. Maybe if you had come, just once, you'd have understood why. When we lose people we love, we need to remember how they lived, not just how they died. Life is more than shadows; it's the light behind*

those shadows. Accidents are just that: accidents. No one and no place is to blame. I had hoped coming back here might help us all to heal and to forgive.

Ari, if you're reading this, it means we never got our summer at the cabin. I sure am sorry about that. Sometimes wanting something, no matter how much, can't make it happen. Exploring Canoe Lake together would have been grand, but I take comfort in knowing that a world of adventure still awaits you.

Mr. Foster has a list of my worldly possessions to be divided up between James and Laurel, but Ari, I want the Canoe Lake property to go to you. Time has run out for me, but I still want you to have an opportunity to discover the magic of our little place in the woods, maybe even put down some roots.

I've set aside enough cash to cover taxes, maintenance and other such costs so you won't have to worry about any of that for several years. If, after trying it, you find that owning land in the bush doesn't suit you, if you don't like it or want it and decide to sell, half the money from the sale will go into a trust fund for you, with the other half split evenly between James and Laurel.

Finally (and what could be more final than this?) and most importantly, I want you to know I love you, the whole lot of you. You're as good a family as a man could ask for.

Look after each other.

Love, Gramps/Pop/Father

His words were so clear that I swear I heard Gramps' voice and felt him beside me with a lake in front of us, the red canoe bobbing in the shallows and our tent pitched in the sand. But I open my eyes, and I'm back in Mr. Foster's office, without Gramps.

"Ari," Mr. Foster says, "do you understand your grandfather's wishes?"

My nose tickles. I wipe it with my hand. My cheeks are wet.

"Ari, all one hundred and sixty acres that your grandfather owned, including the buildings, now belong to you."

"Me?" I practically choke. "The land?"

He nods.

"The cabin?"

He nods again.

"Wh-what do I do with it?"

"That, young man, is up to you," Mr. Foster says.

"You'll sell it, of course." Aunt Laurel tries to laugh but it comes out a cackle. "What could you possibly do with a cabin on raw land in the middle of nowhere? You're far too young to –"

"I'll be thirteen on my next birthday. And thanks to Gramps, I know exactly what to do on that land. We spent hours talking about it on the phone. We made plans to explore Canoe Lake together. And if I can't do that with him, I'll do it for him. That's what he wanted. He said so, right there in his will. You heard him."

"Let's not get ahead of ourselves," Mr. Foster says, looking me straight in the eyes. "You are still underage, Ari, even at thirteen, so there is a condition."

"What condition?" I ask.

"Laurel and James are co-executors of Walter's will, and James is your legal guardian. If both of them agree that selling the property would be in your best interest, they can choose to sell it and follow the trust fund option for you instead."

"They can sell Gramps' place whether I want to or not?"

"Only if they both agree that would be best for you. Do all of you understand?"

Dad, Aunt Laurel and I nod, but my head is reeling. At least one thing I can count on is that Dad and Aunt Laurel never agree on anything.

Mr. Foster stands up and shakes the Mountie's hand. "Thank you for your time, Constable." He then turns to us and says, "Give yourselves some time before you make any big decisions. Take my card, and don't hesitate to call if you have any questions or concerns."

He hands all three of us a card, even me. No one has ever given me a business card before.

With every step out of Mr. Foster's office, more of what Gramps said sinks into my head. By the time I pass the wall mural ladies, I can hear them whispering, "That's Ari Martin. He owns land. He's important."

I smile at them. Something good has finally happened to me. I have my own place, a place where I can do what I want, when I want. Maybe I'll get a dog, a cat, a horse, a cow. Maybe I'll open my own arcade, pizza place or doughnut shop. The possibilities are endless. Gramps spoke to me plain as pie and gave me the biggest, most amazing gift of my whole life.

Dad slumps into the front seat of the car while Aunt Laurel babbles non-stop, something about starting a hair salon where she'll be the boss. Sheesh! I pull down my cap and let my thoughts run free, hardly noticing the bumps and curves in the road.

The cabin is mine. The garden, raspberries, swing, gate – all of it mine. My own place. My own place. I repeat it over and over, chanting as if to cast a spell to protect it.

When we reach Gramps' gate, I take the key and jump out to open it. "No need to wait," I tell Aunt Laurel, slipping the key into my pocket as she drives through. "I'll walk."

I close and lock the gate, but I don't walk. I skip, turn cartwheels, spin in circles with my arms spread wide. Dad and Aunt Laurel go inside, but my happiness is too big for indoors. I head for Gramps' shed. "Look out weeds. Here I come!"

Armed with shovel and work gloves, I set out on a raspberry search and rescue mission in my very own garden. Weeds fall hard and fast.

"Psst!"

I look up from a particularly nasty thistle but see no one. I pull on the thorny stem.

"Pssssst!" Longer this time, louder and more insistent.

Before I can look up, the weed snaps off and I land with a thud on my butt.

"Nice move, jogger boy, very elegant."

"Hey!" I say, louder than I meant to.

"He speaks!" says the voice.

I see only trees, but I recognize the voice of the girl I ran into yesterday. Her head pops out briefly from behind a tree trunk, her wild hair splintering the sunlight. I blink, and she ducks back behind the tree.

"How did you find me?" I ask.

"Again, he speaks, and in sentences!"

"How did you find me?" I repeat.

"I have my ways."

"What ways?"

"Mine. Now let's go. I can't let the Road Hag see me."

"Who?"

"No time to explain. I'm going. Are you coming?" She steps farther into the trees.

CHAPTER FIVE

"WHY WOULD I FOLLOW YOU?" I tell the rustling leaves. "I don't know you."

"Ah, but I know you."

"No you don't."

"You're Ari Martin, Walter's golden grandson. Can we go now?"

"Golden? Me? Where'd you hear that? From Gramps? You knew him? Hey, wait up," I shout to the leaves and branches as they part and close ahead of me.

I follow as best I can, barely keeping up with her. What if she leads me deep into the woods and ditches me, or worse? "Could you at least tell me your name?" My voice has a shrill edge. Will she notice?

She doesn't answer, so I turn back toward the garden.

"Okay, you win. The name's Tamari, like the sauce, but you can call me Tam. That's what I answer to."

"Tam? Tam who?" Did Gramps mention her? He talked about so many people that their names all ran together. They were characters in his stories, not real people.

"Tam What-difference-does-it-make. I'm Tam, you're Ari. Now we know who's who, let's go. Keep talking though. It gives the bears a heads-up that we're coming." She shifts into a higher gear, walking faster and faster.

"Bears?"

"Bears. But don't worry about them. The way you plow through the bush even the trees will want to run and hide."

Branches slap my legs and chest. A twig knocks off my cap – stupid haircut. I scoop it up quickly, not wanting to lose my guide. I step over another log, or is it the same one I passed a few minutes ago? City buildings have numbers or names. But here, how can you tell one tree or bush or rock or log from any other?

A soft sound whispers through the bush. Rushing water? Wind? The brush grows thicker, the ground wetter. My steps squelch noisily. Sometimes my feet push on while my shoes seem to want to stay behind. We start up a gentle slope, and the bog dries up.

Tam stops abruptly and points. "Look, a morel!"

I bump into her. This girl needs warning lights. "Where?" Gramps and I picked morels. I look around but I don't see any mushrooms.

She picks the morel and slips it into her jacket pocket. "Finders keepers," she says. "Now close your eyes. I have a surprise for you."

"And I have a surprise for you. I'm not closing my eyes."

"DO YOU ALWAYS CARRY A BLINDFOLD?" I ask as Tam leads me, groping and stumbling, through a vicious maze of plant life. How did I let her talk me into this?

"Sweat bands have more uses than you might imagine. Out here, you don't have to be a boy scout to be prepared. But maybe golden boys don't worry about stuff like that. Maybe you don't sweat."

Tam talks. I stumble. And through the woods we go.

Suddenly, we stop and she whips off my blindfold.

I blink. Sunlight. Water. I blink again. A long, sandy beach curves around a small, perfect bay. Tiny waves lap the sand and splash against a tall boulder just offshore.

"I'll race you into the water," Tam says.

"What?"

Her jacket, shoes and socks fly off. She drops her pants.

Crimson floods my face and ears.

Tam splashes into the water, wearing only her T-shirt and underwear. "Come on in. You'll love it, guaranteed."

"Um, uh, I...uh, I don't have a – a swimsuit."

"No need, in case you didn't notice. Just think of it as giving your underwear a free wash and an extra day's wear."

I look back at the wall of trees around the beach. Gramps' cabin is back there somewhere. But where?

I sit down, kick off my shoes, peel off my sweaty socks, pull my knees up to my chest and dig my toes into the warm sand.

"Are you waiting for a written invitation?" When I don't move or answer, she says, "If you're worried about getting caught..."

"We're in the middle of nowhere. Who's gonna catch us?"

"The Road Hag. Who else? Everybody, and I mean everybody, steers clear of her. She threatened to call the cops on anyone she catches trespassing, but since I'm with you..."

"What?" I ask the head floating on the water.

"This beach is on your grandfather's land. He invited the whole community to use it, but after he died, the Road Hag built that stupid gate. The ground hadn't even thawed."

"You mean our gate? The steel gate by the main road? The one Aunt Laurel put in?"

"The very one."

"But that's nowhere near here."

"Exactly. Two years ago, Walter extended his driveway from the main road to the bay to make it easier for us locals to come here."

"You call that snarly trail we came in on a driveway?"

"How big a bumpkin do you think I am? Wait, don't answer. Just look over there." She points to a gap in the trees. "Your driveway comes right to this beach. No one calls it your driveway though. We call it Walter's Way."

Tam dives underwater, giving her words time to sink in. When she pops back to the surface, I say, "Couldn't you just ask Aunt Laurel to let you in?" As if I didn't know the answer.

"You think we didn't try? At first we came to pay our respects and see if we could help or find out when Walter's service was, stuff like that. But all she said was 'Go away or I'll report you to the police.' So we left her alone. A few of us blazed the secret trail you and I used, and we threw brush on Walter's Way so Auntie Road Hag wouldn't drive in here and catch us. Now, are you jumping in the lake or not? I'm getting cold."

WE WALK BACK ON WALTER'S WAY. Even with the brush piles, it's faster and easier than the way we came. Tam drips lake water and I drip sweat, having taken too long to get up the nerve to drop my pants in front of her.

A corner of the cabin comes into view. Tam swears me to secrecy about her, the trail, Walter's Way and the beach. Then, just like before, she vanishes into the woods.

Back at the cabin, Dad's sitting on the porch, cradling his guitar and strumming the same three chords over and over. Aunt Laurel, with elbow-length rubber gloves and her tunes plugged into her fairy ears, is scrubbing out a cupboard, sloshing water everywhere. Neither stops to ask me where I've been. Did they even notice I was gone?

CHAPTER SIX

I LIE IN BED UNDER A SKYLIGHT full of stars. After Mom died, Dad hardly opened his eyes for months. Kids at school avoided me as if dead relatives were contagious. I did all the cooking and cleaning, while Aunt Laurel kept calling and telling me to make Dad smarten up and get busy doing things I knew he'd never do. We had to move to a smaller apartment because Dad couldn't or wouldn't get out of bed. And through all that, Gramps called every single day. We had long conversations, sometimes about Dad or Mom, but mostly fun stuff like fishing or swimming or bushwhacking or hockey. Gramps could make me laugh no matter how sad I felt.

Now Gramps is gone, but he gave me this perfect place. And maybe even helped me find a friend, my first new friend in years: Tam.

Ring! Ring!

What the? My dream slips away and I open my eyes to morning. Aunt Laurel says hello and the ringing stops. She sure sounds cheerful.

By the time I get dressed and down the ladder, she's grinning, actually grinning, across her whole face.

"That was Sylvia, the realtor. She's coming tomorrow morning at nine to see the property, and I'd like to have it looking as good as possible before she comes. That means we have a lot to do between now and then."

"What?" I ask. "Why?"

"Yeah," Dad says, looking up from his coffee. "Why bother cleaning? The place is what it is. Busting our buns polishing it won't change it."

"Are you saying what I think you're saying, Aunt Laurel?" All my blood sinks to my feet. "Realtors sell places, and you're having a realtor come here, to sell it?"

"Not right away," she says, still grinning, "but before the property gets any more dilapidated than it already is."

"But you can't sell it! I haven't even had it a whole day yet." Tears sting my eyes. My throat closes so tight I can't swallow.

"Come on, Ari. Be reasonable." Aunt Laurel's grin falls off her face. "Keeping this property isn't practical. Neither I nor your father wants to live here, and you can't stay here by yourself. The place will go to ruin with no one here to look after it. That's why Father gave us the option of selling it and opening a trust fund for you. Believe me. It's for the best."

"The best for who? You? Dad? Not for me. Gramps wanted me to get to live here, not just spend a day or two."

"Relax, Ari," Dad says. "Places like this don't sell overnight. We'll have time this summer to do whatever you want."

"And then go back to our crappy apartment on that crappy street?"

"Life is complicated, Ari," Dad says.

"You're taking Aunt Laurel's side. Why? Why won't you listen to me? You can invite a hundred realtors here and scrub the logs till they're flat as pancakes, but I'm not leaving and you can't make me."

I run out the door before they can throw more excuses at me.

By the time I reach the bay, I'm covered in sweat and grit.

I've probably tripped over fifty sticks and fallen more times than I care to count. I rip my clothes off, underwear included, and dive into the icy water.

The cold sucks my breath away, but I duck my head and swim, rippling the silky lake. My skin tingles. I swim out to the big boulder and keep swimming till I can barely move my arms and legs. When I can't take another stroke, I roll onto my back and float, arms spread, weightless, my heart pounding.

Questions pummel my brain like hailstones. "What can I do? How can I stop Dad and Aunt Laurel? Can I even slow them down?"

"Hey, jogger boy. This is a side of you I haven't seen before."

I flip over and dive deep. Lungs bursting, I have to kick back to the surface. I lift my head and gasp for air.

"I brought my little brother, Evan, for swimming practice. I've been telling him about you." As she speaks, she and Evan undress. Both have swimsuits.

I should swim as fast and far away as I can and never look back, but my tired arms and legs veto that plan, seconded by my shrivelled fingers and toes.

Tam wades into the water ahead of her brother.

"Hey, Ari, watch me swim," Evan calls, grinning. "I'm really good."

I zero in on my clothes, stroking toward them while staying as far as possible from Tam and Evan. Evan puts his face in the water and starts kicking and splashing, his idea of swimming. I swim, then run as fast as I can for shore. Sand grinds my feet with every step, but I don't stop. I grab my clothes and dive into the bush.

CHAPTER SEVEN

"YOU WOULDN'T HAVE TO DO THAT," Tam calls after me, "if you'd taken my laundry advice and kept your underwear on."

My damp T-shirt refuses to dry my cold skin. My skin retaliates by fighting my jeans like an alien invader. Eventually, both skin and clothes settle on a clammy truce.

"Did you see me put my face in the water?" Evan calls. "Did you see how far I swam?"

I sprawl out on the warm sand and watch Tam try to teach her brother to breathe through his mouth and turn his head instead of lifting it straight up.

Bumper car thoughts about my property rumble through my head. Maybe I just need a different perspective, a little space.

"You know where I live," I shout to Tam. "How about showing me where you live?"

"Why not?" Tam yells back. "We're headed there anyway after our lesson."

After they dry off, we bash our way through the bush trail till we reach the main road. They pull their bikes out from behind a tree.

Still in instructor mode, Tam says, "Ari, you pedal. I'll ride on the handlebars and tell you where to go."

I pedal through the valley, up hills and down. Tam jumps off at a wooden gate. On the other side, several cows graze in a large field.

"This gate is to keep milk cows in," she says, "not neighbours out. See? No lock."

Evan pedals past us, feet flying. I push the bike inside and wait while Tam closes the gate behind us, careful to keep her and the bike between me and the cows.

She leads me to a small purple house with green trim.

"You wanted to see where I live. Well, here we are." She opens the door into a small room with coat hooks, shoes and boots.

The warm scent of fresh bread welcomes us. In Toronto, bakeries have this heavenly smell, but no homes I can remember since Mom died.

"No outside shoes in the house," Tam instructs.

"I thought only Japanese people did that."

"Welcome to Japan."

I kick off my shoes and follow her into the kitchen, where I'm greeted by a backside bent over the oven. The bent figure is using the apron tied around its narrow waist to remove a golden loaf of bread. I expect to see Tam's mother, but when the figure turns, its face is covered with a full, dark beard.

"Perfect timing, Tam," the man says, adding, "Hope you like fresh bread, Ari."

"How do you know my name?" I say. "Did Evan tell you I was here?"

"Nope, he headed straight for the shower. You just happen to fit Walter's description of you."

"Ari," Tam says, "this is my mom's friend Ben. He's staying here while she's away planting trees."

"Pleased to meet you, Ari." Ben empties the bread onto a rack. "Though from all Walter told us, I feel I already know you. Sorry about his passing. He was quite a man." He reaches into the oven for a second loaf.

Inside a box by the oven, an orange mother cat stretches and curls around three tiny balls of fur. She meows again and licks her babies gently. I kneel beside her.

"Want one?" Tam asks.

I touch the smallest kitten, black with white paws – so, so soft. Mama lifts her head, and I pull back my hand.

"You like the runt?" she says. I nod. "Perfect. The other two already have homes. Three more weeks, plus time for Miss Marmalade to teach her to mouse, and she's all yours."

"Mine?" I've never even had a goldfish.

"How about some bread?" Ben says. "It's still too hot to slice, but the ends will be nice and crunchy with butter and some of your favourite raspberry jam."

"How do you know I like raspberry jam?"

Ben bows. "Meet Walter's partner in jam. We picked and ate fruit by the truckload. What we didn't eat fresh, we made into jam, jelly, wine, pie filling, chutney...you name it, we tried it. But most of the raspberry jam we sent to you and your dad."

"You helped Gramps with our CARE packages?"

"Walter and I made quite the team."

But me and Gramps were a team. We were best friends *and* family. Sure he talked about his friends, but I'm his only grandson. I'm the one he chose to give his land to.

Ben puts plates on the table, each with a slab of hot bread slathered with a thick layer of butter and jam. He takes a guitar off one of the chairs and leans it against the wall before he sits down.

"You play guitar?" I ask.

"Whenever I can," Ben says. "My friends and I play in a band."

"My dad has a guitar, but he's just learning," I say. "He isn't very good yet."

"If he likes it, he'll get better," Ben says. "Now let's eat."

The rich brown bread is soft and crunchy at the same time, dripping with raspberries and butter. I take another bite and another, chewing and swallowing, chewing and swallowing.

When I open my mouth for my next bite, the words slip out. "Gramps gave me his cabin and his land." The words won't stop. "Me! I own all of it. It's mine."

"Right on!" Ben says. "Walter told me he wanted to do that."

"He did?"

"He said life had kicked you around like a soccer ball, and more than anything he wanted you to have a chance to know something better."

"But a realtor is coming tomorrow. Dad and Aunt Laurel can sell and bounce me right out of here. I don't know what to do."

"Slow down a minute and breathe," Ben says. "Maybe Laurel and James are just trying to be responsible. Finding out what the place is worth doesn't necessarily mean they plan to sell it."

"Aunt Laurel wants to sell. She said so."

"And your dad, what does he want?" Ben asks.

I hesitate, trying to remember exactly what Dad said.

"Talk to him," Ben says.

"Do you know my dad?" I ask.

"I planned to meet him and spend some time with all your family when you came three years ago, but after that terrible accident with the logging truck, well, you know. I'm so sorry about what happened to your mom."

"I should go," I say, not wanting to hear any more.

"You want me to come with you? When your aunt got here, she was hurting and didn't want to deal with strangers. But now a little more time has passed. Both she and your dad might want to hear about how big a part of our community Walter was," Ben says.

"Maybe," I say, "but not today. Not yet."

"Later, perhaps," he says. "I'm happy to help any way I can. Meanwhile, how about a ride home?"

"Thanks, but I'd rather walk," I say. "I need time to think."

"You can borrow my bike," Tam says. "Leave it in the bush by your gate, and we'll pick it up later."

I finish my bread, then squat down to see my kitten before I go. I stroke mama cat's back till she purrs and closes her eyes. With my other hand, I reach down to tickle my tiny kitten's tummy.

We say our goodbyes, and Tam says, "Turn left after you close the gate and stay on the main road till you get to your place on the right."

As the door clicks shut behind me, I remember the cows I passed on my way in. The fingers of my right hand curl into a fist, ready to knock on the now closed door and ask Tam to walk me to the gate.

Seriously? A bodyguard *for cows?* Cows, not lions not tigers not bears.

I grab Tam's bike and place it between me and the cows. Muscles tensed, jaw clenched and heart pounding, I start walking.

CHAPTER EIGHT

IF THE GATE WERE OPEN, I'd jump on the bike and be gone, but, of course, it isn't.

Four black cows stand between me and the gate – closer, not farther, than before. I bow my legs, cowboy casual, and walk. The cows chew their cud and swish their tails. One raises her head and follows me with her eyes. The others ignore me.

When I reach the gate, I push the bike through, and in seconds I'm pedaling down the road.

"Yeehaw!" I shout. "Ari Martin, cow whisperer!"

I pedal fast with the wind on my skin.

This visit to Canoe Lake is so different from my first one, and not all the ways are sad or bad. Last time, Mom made sure someone kept at least two eyes on me at all times. I wasn't allowed to sleep in the loft because Mom worried I might fall. Gramps packed plenty of fishing, swimming, berry picking, paddling and just plain fun into those few days before the accident, but I never had freedom like this to go where I want, when I want, as fast as I want.

In Toronto I come and go, but the buildings, streets, traffic and crowds of people exist in some other solar system. Here trees outnumber everything. Even the smells are different.

No wonder Gramps loved it.

I stash Tam's bike in the bush outside our gate.

Dad's on the front porch, whittling his piece of wood. I still have no idea what it is, but it's pointy on both ends. Aunt Laurel steps outside, letting the screen door slam behind her. Dad looks up.

"This running away has to stop, young man," Aunt Laurel says.

"We worry about you," Dad says.

"Sure you do."

Dad's face actually takes on some colour. "What if something happened to you? How would we find you?"

"I can take care of myself," I say. "I've done it for years."

"That was mean," Dad says.

"And also true."

"If it were up to me, Ari, you'd be grounded, but that's your father's call." Aunt Laurel gives Dad an icy look. He shrugs. "You've had your little outing, now make yourself useful. That garden needs more work."

"Why?" Dad says. "For every weed he pulls, twenty more will grow."

"I just thought someone besides me might lift a finger around here for a change," Aunt Laurel says. "James, I'm still waiting for you to fix that leaky tap in the kitchen and my wonky dresser drawer and the light in the bathroom and..."

"Lifting a finger, now there's an idea," Dad says. "Ari and I will gladly lift our fingers – our whole arms in fact. We're going fishing."

"Fishing?" the word explodes from Aunt Laurel's mouth.

"Pop had gear. I know he did. Have you seen it, Sis?"

"There's some in the garden shed," I say. "I'll go get it."

Aunt Laurel stomps back into the house with a growl fierce enough to frighten a grizzly.

What just happened? Instead of getting in trouble for taking off and mouthing off, I'm going fishing. Fishing!

I unlatch the shed door, take two long steps, grab the fishing poles from the corner, turn and run back out. Smack into Dad.

"Two poles. Good. Did you see a tackle box? Pop had all kinds of fishing gear," he says, stepping around me into the shed. He looks around and a shadow falls over him. "This must be exactly how Pop left it," he whispers.

"I don't see a tackle box, so let's not waste time looking for one. We have fish to catch." I speak quickly before Dad's black hole swallows him again. "These poles have hooks, and here are a couple of trowels. Let's go dig some worms."

Dad grabs a bucket. "We can put our worms in here, and after we catch our dinner we can rinse out the bucket and use it to carry our fish home."

"For Aunt Laurel to fry," I say.

"That'll be the day," Dad says.

He follows me into the sunshine. I start digging beside the shed, but Dad keeps walking.

"Over here," he calls. "Better to liberate raspberries than waste time on random weed attacks."

"How do you know where the raspberries are?"

"I helped Pop plant them the summer he bought this place. I was a teenager so I wasn't keen to work in the dirt, but after our first crop of ripe raspberries, I became their chief caretaker."

"Did you spend a lot of time here?" I ask, hoping to stir up happy memories.

"Not a lot," Dad says as we pull weeds then pluck worms from the loose dirt. "As you know, your grandmother lost interest in this place after she stepped on that wasp nest. And who could blame her, allergic as she was? Rustic living just wasn't her thing, so after living here less than a year, we moved back to the city. That was the end of it for Mom and Laurel, but Pop and I came up every summer until I graduated high school. Then I got busy doing other things, and I never came again until that last time with you and your mom."

Uh-oh, blues alert.

I point to a cluster of tiny green berries. "When do you think they'll be ripe?"

"Not for a while," Dad says.

"Imagine pigging out on sweet, juicy berries again. That's worth waiting for, eh, Dad?"

We work in silence, freeing raspberry bushes and capturing worms until the dirt in our small bucket squirms like Medusa's head.

"Where now?" I ask. "The lake?"

"Rainbow Creek. We can walk there, and it's positively thick with trout. Pop had a trail. This way, I think." Dad picks up the worm bucket and hands me a pole.

We set off at right angles to Walter's Way.

"I don't remember a creek," I say as we tractor our way through the bush.

"That's because when you were here we took the canoe to the lake. We never got to the creek."

Branches slap us, sticks trip us, but Dad plows ahead. Is he humming? If this place can make Dad that happy, we've *got* to keep it.

Ducking under a low leaning tree, I thread my pole through yet another prickly maze, trying to keep up with a man who gets lost in shopping malls.

CHAPTER NINE

"LET'S SIT FOR A MINUTE," Dad says, flopping onto a fallen log. "I'm a bit out of shape for hiking."

No kidding, I want to say but instead I sit quietly beside him.

As his breathing slows, I say, "Gramps was sure happy here, wasn't he?"

Dad half smiles.

"Maybe if we lived here we could be happy."

Dad shrugs.

"People talk about fresh starts, you know, how important they are and all, especially after something terrible happens like it did to us. I could never picture you and me having fun or feeling happy again until Gramps gave me this land. But now, as fresh starts go, what could be fresher than forests, mountains, lakes, Rainbow Creek? Gramps set everything up for us here. All we have to do is stay."

Dad shrugs again. "Life isn't that simple," he says, "but now isn't the time for philosophy, now's the time for fishing. Wait till you see Pop's fishing hole. It's the prettiest place on earth."

"Are we close?" I ask, still catching my breath from all those words.

Dad picks up his pole and the worm bucket and starts walking. "Can't be far now."

I stand up to follow him and see a slice of white and purple dangling from a branch a fair ways back. My cap!

"Coming, Ari?" Dad asks.

Pointing, I say, "See my Rockies cap way over there? Can we make our path wide enough from here to the creek so I can find it on our way back?"

"No problem," Dad says, crashing ahead. "If this isn't Pop's old trail, we can sure as sugar make ourselves a new trail."

I grab my pole and join the crashing.

Snapping twigs, bashing bushes, stacking rocks: snap, bash, crash, stack, over and over again. James and Ari Martin, trailblazers.

"Listen, Ari, the creek!" Dad yells. "We must be nearly there."

We stop on a steep cliff overlooking a wide, burbling creek.

"Upstream or down?" Dad says, as much to himself as to me. "Which way to Pop's secret spot? Hard to tell with these trees blocking our view. I know it's on the other side of the creek. There was some sort of rock bridge we crossed."

A cloud of mosquitoes buzzes us into action.

"Why don't we start fishing and see where we end up?" I point upstream. "Looks like we can get down to the water over there."

"Watch out trout. Here we come," Dad says. "Lead the way, Son."

We add slipping and sliding to our bashing and crashing, throw in a few scratches, a new bruise or two, and we reach the creek.

Dad pinches a couple of worms onto our hooks and we're good to go. Except for one thing. I haven't a clue how to fish.

The last time I went fishing, which was also my first time, all I did was hold the pole. Gramps did everything else. He hooked a giant trout on his line and let me reel it in. Man, that fish could fight! If I remember correctly, he brought the pole back behind him to cast into the water. I ease my pole back and immediately hook a branch.

Unhooking me, Dad says, "No need to cast here like we did at the lake; only fly fishers cast in streams. With worms you just loosen your line like this and let the current carry it downstream. Before it drifts too far, reel it back in, slowly."

He walks upstream, leaving me a nice ripply spot.

I drop my line into the water, let the current carry it, then reel it back in, just like Dad told me. Drop, wait, reel, repeat.

The worm swims in, the worm swims out, if I get lucky I'll catch a trout.

I'm watching my line glide downstream when a distant shadow catches my eye. Someone else fishing? This far in the bush?

The shadow moves. Closer. Someone's fishing, all right, but this fisher has no rod, no reel, no bait. And no clothes.

A black bear wades toward us, his nose to the water.

I drop my pole and yell, "Bear!"

Dad looks up, sees the bear, and we take off, splashing and panting, running upstream as fast and far from the bear as we can go. With my heart thudding and blood practically squirting out my ears, we duck behind the first big rock we see then peek over the top.

The bear wades deeper into the water, turns his head slowly upstream, then down, up, down, up...SNAP!

His head splashes underwater then rises up high. A silvery fish dangles from his jaws. He gives his head a sharp shake then lumbers off, carrying his catch into the trees behind him.

We wait behind the rock, soaking wet and shivering, trying to catch our breath.

"That bear could be anywhere," I say. "He could have friends. Lots of friends."

"Or *he* could be a *she*, with cubs to protect," Dad says. "I don't know about you, but I've had enough fun fishing for today."

"Let's grab our poles and get out of here," I say.

We edge our way back to where we were fishing, expecting every bush and rock to turn into a hungry bear. The tip is broken on Dad's pole, but he packs it up as best he can. I scan the creek for mine, but it's gone missing. Maybe the bear can use it.

We slog along on numb feet, our pant legs soaked.

"Lucky you lost your cap," Dad says. "Without that trail, we could wander for hours and still not find our way home."

We wade through slippery shallows. Icy water pushes against the backs of our legs. Our eyes and ears catch every shadow, every sound.

The slope away from the creek seems steeper going up. I take a deep breath, swallow hard and start climbing. After scrabbling up a few steps, I lose my momentum and start to slide back. With every muscle, I push, grabbing at branches, rocks, anything that might hold me. Dad stumbles along behind. My foot slips, setting off a cascade of pebbles.

Adrenalin boosts me to the top. Then I turn and coax Dad. "To your right," I call. "See that root? Grab it. Good. Now aim for that mossy rock. Okay, now..."

Broken branch by broken branch, we follow our trail. In the distance I see my cap!

The farther we go, the faster we move, slapping branches, tripping on sticks, kicking stones faster, faster.

I rescue my cap and start singing, *"Today's the day we won't be the teddy bears' pic – nic."*

Dad joins the chorus. *"Picnic time for teddy bears."*

When we reach the garden, I throw my arms in the air and pump my fists. "Wow, I just saw my first bear, a real live wild you-better-believe-it big black hairy bear! Ho – ly snort."

"Lucky for us, Smokey preferred take-away to dining in," Dad says.

"Maybe Smokey should be our little secret," I say. "If we tell Aunt Laurel, she might lock us in the cabin forever."

Dad actually smiles.

We're halfway up the porch steps when Aunt Laurel swings open the screen. "What, no fish?" she says.

"Oh, but you should see the one that got away," Dad says.

"Yeah, he took my pole," I say.

Dad looks at his hands. "Oops," he says. "That fish was so hungry he took our bait *and* the bucket."

"Good," Aunt Laurel says. "We can't stink up the house before the realtor comes."

CHAPTER TEN

LAST NIGHT, Dad spent more time grilling Aunt Laurel about Gramps' fishing gear than she spent grilling mushroom/grape tomato/yellow pepper/onion kebabs.

"What about those good fly rods?" Dad asked. "And Pop's hand-tied flies? I'm sure he had a tackle box. He had way better gear than what we found in that garden shed. Where is it? Have you seen it?"

Dad nagged on, but Aunt Laurel went cryptic, saying things like, "All in good time" and "What's with the sudden interest in fishing?"

All night long, I tossed in my bed, tearing my brain apart, searching for that flash of brilliance that would save my new home. But all I got were stars light years away, blinking their indifference.

The sun has barely hit the sky when Aunt Laurel yells through my thin sleep, "Ari, run and open the gate for Sylvia, will you? We want to be ready when she comes."

"Open the gate yourself," I grumble, still half asleep.

"I thought that woman was coming at nine," Dad says. "That's two hours from now."

"Realtors are busy people. We can't forget the gate and keep her waiting," Aunt Laurel says.

"Don't ask for my help," I say. "I'm not the one who invited her."

"But you *are* the one with the key," Aunt Laurel reminds me.

And so I am. I scrounge around and find the key, but I refuse to pull a puppy dog and do as I'm told. "You know, Aunt Laurel, this is my property, and I don't have to open the gate if I don't want to."

"James, speak to your son. Now isn't the time for games."

"This is no game," I say. "You're messing with my future."

Aunt Laurel lets loose a sigh that would flatten two little piggies' houses. I pull on shorts and a T-shirt, then climb down the ladder with the key to the gate in my pocket. At the bottom of the ladder, I pull out the key and hold it in front of Aunt Laurel who has deflated into a chair.

"Here's the deal," I say. "I'll open the gate if you'll hope-to-die swear you won't let that realtor put up any for sale signs."

"It's much too soon to worry about for sale signs," Dad says. "The realtor has to look the place over and give us an estimate of what it's worth before we start talking about selling."

Aunt Laurel heaves another sigh. "Estimates are standard procedure with inheritances. Don't make me the bad guy. I lost my father and I'm grieving just like you. Try to remember that."

"So you're only getting an estimate today? Nothing else?" I say. "Promise me? Both of you?"

I get both of their promises before I leave my cabin to walk down my driveway to open my gate for their realtor.

Once the gate is open, an idea strikes me. The realtor isn't coming for two hours. I have plenty of time for a quick swim at my beach. Breakfast can wait. I run to the garden shed to stash the gate key. I can't risk losing it in the lake.

In a back corner of the shed, I find a tin. Inside it is a

wooden canoe paddle key ring with one key. A key to what? No time for guessing now. The lake calls. I add my key to the tin, put the tin back where I found it, close the shed door and hit Walter's Way at a full run, gaining speed with every step.

Before I see the beach, I hear laughter and an unfamiliar voice yelling, "Look out below!" followed by a huge splash.

"Not bad," Tam's voice yells, "but watch this." Another loud splash.

"What the...?" I run to the end of the road. Towels and backpacks litter the beach. Three heads bob in the water. Two belong to Tam and Evan; the other one is new.

"Hey, look," Evan calls. "It's Ari."

"Ari? As in Walter's perfect grandson?" the new boy says. My face flames.

"Come on in," Evan yells. "The water's perfect."

"Yeah, come jump off Big Boldy with me," the new boy calls. "I'll show you the easy way up."

"You don't have to jump if you don't want to," Evan says. "It's scary high."

Tam splashes out of the water.

"Who's that kid?" I ask when she catches up to me. "And what's he doing here?"

"That's Justin. His family has lived here forever. And we're taking our Wednesday morning wake-up swim. What does it look like?"

"I can see you're swimming, but – but..."

"But what?" Tam says.

"I didn't know you were here," I say.

"So?"

"So this is my beach and I should know who's using it."

"Why? Is that what the Road Hag told you?"

"No."

"Do you expect us to stop by your cabin and ask permission every time we come here?"

"No, it's just that this beach is mine and..."

"Here's a little lesson. A beach is a beach – a part of nature and no one owns nature. Not you, not me, not anyone. This beach was here before us and it will be here after us. We can care for it, but it doesn't belong to us. Plant a garden if you want to call something yours. Gardens need people. Beaches don't. That's what Walter said."

"Don't tell me what my grandfather said. I knew him better and longer than you ever did. Take your stupid lectures and shut up."

Tam's mouth drops open, but before she says another word, Evan shouts from the water, "Hey, Ari, what are you waiting for? Come on in."

"Yeah, let's jump off Boldy," the new boy shouts. "Come on. It's fun."

I turn away from Tam, toss my T-shirt onto the sand, pull off my shoes and socks and dive into the lake in my shorts.

The icy water numbs me through and through before I kick to the surface and swim out to the boulder.

"By the way, I'm Justin," the new boy says as he leads me to the top of the rock. "Now jump," he says. "Hurry. It gets cold up here."

"You first."

"Okay, if you in – sss-sist." He cannonballs off the boulder and hits the lake with a loud *smack!*, shooting a circle of water high in the air.

When he pops back to the surface, he and Evan look up at me from the water – far, far below. Where's Tam? A chill breeze brushes my skin. Rough rock scrapes my feet. I squeeze my eyes shut, take a deep breath, pinch my nose, and step over the edge.

My feet hit the water first and torpedo me deep below the surface. I kick my way back up and burst into the bright sunlight, gasping for air. Evan and Justin cheer like I'm some sort of hero. Tam sits on the beach, wrapped in a towel. Silent.

I climb Big Boldy again. This time the jump is easier, more fun.

I keep jumping and swimming until, shivering, goose-bumped and shrivelled, my soggy body reaches its limit. I need heat. Leaping from a boulder works as a talk and question dodger, but only for so long.

The other kids sit in a row, wrapped in warm towels on the warm sand. "You sure do like jumping," Evan says. "Now Tam can teach you to dive."

I look at Tam, who looks away. I flop down on the sand behind her and close my eyes. Warm sun above me, warm sand below.

Suddenly Evan jumps up and says, "Great gobs of guacamole, I almost forgot my guitar lesson. Come on, Tam, we gotta go."

"Oh, no!" I say. The realtor. "I forgot! I have to go, too." I grab my shirt, shoes and socks and start running.

"Whatever you do, don't tell the Road Hag we were here," Tam yells after me.

Sharp rocks and sticks poke and scratch the bottoms of my feet until I have to stop to pull on my shoes. Walter's Way may be wide, but it isn't smooth. I tug my tee over my head, shoving my arms into the sleeves as I go.

I see the realtor's red car before I see her standing on the far side of it, talking to Dad and Aunt Laurel. She looks up.

"Looks like someone's coming from the beach," she says.

"Beach?" Aunt Laurel says.

"Ari?" Dad says.

"Good to meet you, Ari," says the realtor. "I'm Sylvia."

"And I'm not selling," I tell her.

Sylvia smiles weakly and says, "Well, that's about all I need for today. I'll get back to you as soon as I can with an estimate. Try to track down the key to that building. I'd like to look inside. It might be more than just a storage shed. A potential shop or garage could increase the property value significantly."

"What shop? What garage?" I say.

Sylvia climbs into her car, turns it around and, before she drives away, says, "Looks like more company coming."

CHAPTER ELEVEN

A DUST-COVERED PICKUP pulls over in the driveway to let Sylvia's car pass. An older woman climbs out. "Good morning to you," she says as she reaches back into her truck for a basket that she hangs from the crook of her elbow and a small dog that she carries in her arms. She kicks the truck door shut with her foot.

"I'm Millie Marshall," she says. "I was a friend of Walter's. And this is my Chihuahua, Peppy. We live down the road."

"Good morning, Ms. Marshall," Dad says. "What can we do for you?"

"You must be James, and that one's Laurel. I seen her a few weeks ago," Millie says. "And this young man must be Ari."

"Correct on all counts," Aunt Laurel says. "Now we have everyone's name, what is it you want, Ms. Marshall?"

"Call me Millie. We don't stand on formalities around here. May I come in?"

Dad leads her into the house. Aunt Laurel and I follow, not knowing what else to do.

Millie places Peppy gently on the floor. "Don't worry about him. He's had his breakfast, but I could sure use a cup of tea." She settles into a chair at the table and continues: "I was on my way to Henry and Eileen's when I seen your gate was open. I was taking them this nice batch of ginger-blueberry scones, fresh baked this morning and still warm from the oven. I guess their loss is your gain. I'll put them on a plate, if you have one."

Aunt Laurel takes a serving plate from the cupboard. Dad fills the kettle. I sit beside Millie. Peppy jumps into my lap.

"Anyway, I seen that open gate and decided it was high time I came in and paid my respects. I can take scones to the Washburns any time. Oh, don't bother about butter and cream. I brought some, graciously provided by Roberta, my cow. Bertie gives the sweetest milk in the country, you know."

Aunt Laurel sets the table with mugs, plates, spoons and knives. Dad takes out teabags. Peppy gnaws on my knuckle while Millie arranges her scones on the serving plate.

"You don't remember me, do you?" Millie says, pausing for the first time to wait for an answer. "I didn't think so," she continues. "James, you were just a bratty teenager when I saw you last. You and your dad bought milk and eggs from me. And one time you helped butcher some of my old laying hens. Remember that?"

Dad winces.

"Yep, you made the same face back then. Never helped gather eggs neither, after that one little hen chased you from her nest."

Dad turns up the heat on the kettle and studies it with great intensity.

"And you, Missy," she says to Aunt Laurel, "you and your mama only came here once, but I'll never forget how you loved that garden."

"Wait a minute," I say. "Aunt Laurel? Loved a garden?"

Aunt Laurel's face goes all dreamy. Her eyes shine. Then she clears her throat and says, "Scone, Millie? They're getting cold."

Millie takes a scone and reaches for the butter. The kettle whistles and Dad busies himself with making tea. Then both he and Aunt Laurel sit down. Peppy bounces himself out of my lap and into Millie's.

Millie turns her attention to me. "Of course, young Ari wouldn't remember me because we never met. I planned on having you and your family over for supper that time you visited, but...such an awful tragedy about your mother. I never had a chance to tell all of you how truly sorry I am for your loss."

"Thank you," Dad murmurs.

"And now we've lost Walter, too." Millie feeds Peppy a bite of buttered scone. "Such a shame and such a shock, him going out the way he did. Shovelling snow off his porch after a late spring blizzard. Who'd have guessed? A genuine gentleman he was, and as fine a neighbour as a person could ask for."

"Thank you," Dad murmurs again. Aunt Laurel starts filling mugs with tea.

"It's a real tribute to him to have his family move into his cabin like this and preserve his legacy. He'd be so pleased, and I'm sure you'll all be happy living here."

"Oh." Aunt Laurel spills a puddle of tea on the table. "Oh, no. We're not staying."

"Why not?" Millie asks.

"Well, well," Aunt Laurel sputters, "there are all kinds of reasons. Tell her, James."

Dad sets his mug on the table. "Um, well," he says, "too many sad memories here for me and Ari. And Laurel is planning to open her own hair salon in Vancouver."

"Pshaw," Millie says. "The best cure for sad memories is to make some happy ones. And as for you, Laurel, you're a hairdresser, right?"

Aunt Laurel nods.

"Those fancy streaks in your hair, you done 'em yourself?"

Another nod.

"Very chic, especially with them fairy thingies danglin' from your earlobes."

Aunt Laurel stares.

"We been needing a hairdresser in Canoe Lake forever, and I mean for – ever. I'd be more than happy to trade you haircuts for butter, cream, all sorts of things. Town time is far too precious to waste stuck in front of a mirror in some stinky barbershop. And for all my years of trying, I still can't cut two hairs the same length."

Aunt Laurel does a first-rate impression of a dying fish gasping for air.

"So there you go. Laurel opens her shop here, Ari signs up for our local school. And you –" Millie turns to Dad – "I'm sure you could think of something to do, too."

CHAPTER TWELVE

AFTER WE SAY GOODBYE to Millie and thank her for her scones and don't forget to send along our thanks to Bertie the cow for her butter and cream, we collapse in the living room. Tornado survivors.

If I was younger and Dad and Aunt Laurel were older, we'd take a nap. Instead we simply sit in silence and let the day's events roll around the room like farts in a school cafeteria.

Dad breaks the spell when he gets up to retrieve his wood and starts gouging it for all he's worth.

"What did Sylvia mean when she said you must be coming from the beach?" Aunt Laurel asks me.

Uh-oh. "I don't know what made her say that," I say, trying to sound casual.

"Maybe it had something to do with the new aerial photo she had of the area," Dad says without missing a beat in his gouging. "She said she'd studied it carefully before she came. That's how she knew about the building you didn't tell me about, Sis. Why don't you track down that key so Ari and I can take a look inside?"

"The key can wait," Aunt Laurel says. "Let's check out the beach first."

Oh no. Even if Tam and company aren't there, the place could be crawling with people. A wild bikini beach party. Aunt Laurel would go nuts.

Exactly.

"We could pack a picnic," I say. And why not? If Aunt Laurel finds people there, she'll chase them away and my beach will be private again. If Tam is there, she'll think I came to protect her from the Road Hag, who found out about the beach from the realtor, not me. Perfect.

"I'll make sandwiches," Aunt Laurel says. "James, mix up some lemonade and get the spare blanket from the closet in my room. Ari, go lock the gate. We've had enough visitors for one day."

I lock the gate and return to the cabin as Dad and Aunt Laurel load the last of the picnic items and Dad's guitar into the car.

"Take the front seat, Ari," Dad says, "so you can tell your aunt where to go."

"With pleasure," I say, "on both counts." I don't think Aunt Laurel heard that last part.

The car lurches and bounces over potholes that I never even noticed on foot. We stop at the first brush pile.

"What kind of road is this?" Aunt Laurel asks.

"It almost looks like someone put that brush there intentionally," Dad says.

"Probably just something Gramps didn't get to," I say. "I'll move it in no time."

I jump out of the car and start untangling branches and throwing them aside. Dad and Aunt Laurel wait patiently but don't offer any help. How many of these piles are there?

When the path is clear, I get back in the car. Dad is whistling: *So wide you can't get around it.*

"I didn't know you could whistle," I say.

"I'd pretty much forgotten myself," he says. "Guess it's like riding a bike, eh? Pop taught me both when I was a kid."

Maybe Millie's right. Maybe we *can* live here. Maybe this is exactly what Gramps wanted: a family doing family things, together. I start whistling myself as I untangle the next two piles. A family picnic.

At the end of the road, Aunt Laurel gasps and slams on the brakes. "This...this...this is the bay. I've been here, but I forgot how beautiful it is."

Dad and I take out the picnic makings.

"Come on, Sis. Come sit with us."

Did he actually tell his sister to come and sit? Would fetch be next?

"I had no idea Father's driveway came this far," she says.

"You never checked it out?" Dad asks.

"I was too busy. All that cleaning and sorting and clearing out the cabin and..."

"Okay, okay, we get it, Sis. That's one road we have been down – many, many times."

An osprey sailing on the wind drops with a loud splash into the lake. Wings spread, it rises again, a fish clasped in its talons. A loon calls. Another answers.

We spread the blanket on the sand. Dad passes around sandwiches and lemonade.

A dragonfly lands on Aunt Laurel's shoulder. I cringe, expecting shrieks and flailing arms. But she sits perfectly still. "Dragonflies bring magic when they land on you," she says, adding in the softest of whispers, "fairy magic. Father always said."

The dragonfly deposits its magic and flies away. Loon calls echo back and forth. Water laps the shore. Dad takes out his guitar and plinks the strings to tune it.

For the tiniest moment we're a normal family again. Like our picnics at Bluffer's Beach with Mom's yummy fried chicken, pickles, watermelon and her special chocolate pecan cookies. After swimming and eating, Mom and Dad used to read on the blanket while I built castles in the sand.

CHAPTER THIRTEEN

HO-O-O-O-O-O-O-O-NK! HONK! HONK! HONK! HO-O-O-O-O-O-O-O-NK!

Ear-splitting honking shakes me awake. What? Mating moose? A million geese? A galactic traffic jam? Where am I?

I open my eyes in my bed in the loft. The racket rattles through my window. Below me, Dad and Aunt Laurel skitter around like cockroaches.

"What's going on?" I call down the ladder as I pull on my clothes.

HO-O-O-O-O-O-O-O-NK! HONK! HONK! HONK! HO-O-O-O-O-O-O-NK!

The screen door slams, then slams again.

"Some fool in a truck is blaring his horn outside our gate," Dad shouts as he walks back to the porch.

"Ignore him and he'll go away," Aunt Laurel shouts back.

HO-O-O-O-O-O-O-O-NK! HONK! HONK! HONK! HO-O-O-O-O-O-O-NK!

I join them outside. Together, we ignore him and he doesn't go away. My eardrums beg for mercy.

HO-O-O-O-O-O-O-O-NK! HONK! HONK! HONK! HO-O-O-O-O-O-O-NK!

"Go see what he wants," Aunt Laurel tells Dad.

"Go see yourself," Dad says. "You're the one who installed the gate."

HO-O-O-O-O-O-O-O-NK! HONK! HONK! HONK! HO-O-O-O-O-O-O-NK!

"We'll both go," Aunt Laurel says.

HO-O-O-O-O-O-O-O-NK! HONK! HONK! HONK! HO-O-O-O-O-O-O-NK!

Arm in arm, they disappear down the driveway.

The honking stops. I wait for Dad and Aunt Laurel. I wait longer. Have they been kidnapped? What should I do?

They return, moving fast. "Go and open the gate, Ari," Aunt Laurel shouts. "Mr. Wagner is waiting."

"Who's Mr. Wagner?" I ask. "Am I supposed to know him?"

"Hurry up. We don't have all day," Aunt Laurel says before she runs into the house. Dad follows.

This gatekeeper job is getting old. I do as I'm told, but I don't hurry. I stroll over to the shed, retrieve the key from its tin and mosey up the driveway.

I open the gate, and Mr. Wagner drives through, leaving me in a cloud of dust. He never even looked at me. His fancy silver pickup had a logo on the side. Mountain Properties? Probably another realtor. Dad and Aunt Laurel will send him away soon enough. I prop open the gate so as not to slow down his exit and drop the key in my pocket.

He parks so close to the porch that he opens his truck door onto the steps. His feet never touch the dirt. He's dressed for downtown: fancy suit, tie, briefcase, the works. Aunt Laurel whisks him into the cabin.

What's a man like that doing in a place like this?

The logo on the truck's passenger door reads *Mountain Properties: A Vision for the Future. J.P. Wagner, President.* I step onto the running board to peek inside.

BEEP, BEEP, BEEP

Before I can move, Mr. Wagner runs out of the cabin. "Stop! Step away from that truck! I'm warning you. Don't touch it." He slips his right hand into his jacket pocket.

BEEP, BEEP, BEEP

Dad and Aunt Laurel run out behind him. "What's going on?" Dad shouts.

BEEP, BEEP, BEEP

"Move away from the truck now, you little punk," the man yells. "I won't warn you again."

BEEP, BEEP, BEEP

I swallow. My toes root into the ground.

BEEP, BEEP, BEEP

"Stop that ridiculous alarm," Dad yells, grabbing the man's arm. "My son won't hurt your truck."

BEEP, BEEP, BEEP

Mr. Wagner pulls out his key ring, clicks it, and the alarm stops. "Your son? What's your son doing with my truck?"

"Nothing," Dad says. "He probably just brushed it with his shirt sleeve as he was walking by. No harm done."

"Well, stay away from my truck, kid."

"No problem, Mr. Wagner," Aunt Laurel says. "Run along and play, Ari, or go pull weeds or whatever. Just steer clear of Mr. Wagner's truck."

Run along and play? Like a four-year-old? I stare at them.

"Go on, Ari. It's okay," Dad says. "We won't be long."

Okay my big toe. As soon as they're back inside, I slink around the side of the truck and quietly climb the porch steps. Rats! The screen *and* the door are shut. I can't hear or see a thing. Hugging the logs, I inch my way toward the window and peek inside.

They're huddled around the kitchen table, studying something, their backs to me. Mr. Wagner is pointing to that something. If Tam were here, she'd know what to do.

I head for the garden, avoiding the stupid truck.

The raspberries are still green. I pull weeds, hoping for a friendly *Pssst!* Many weeds later and still no Tam.

My stomach reminds me I haven't had breakfast. Maybe if I go inside, Mr. Wagner will take the hint and leave.

On my way back to the cabin, the screen door slams and Mr. Wagner's voice booms across the yard, "No need to walk around the property. I've seen the aerial photo."

"Don't you want to see the new outbuilding?" Dad says.

"All these buildings will have to come down," Mr. Wagner says, "so seeing them really isn't necessary."

All three of them are now standing on the porch.

"What buildings?" I shout. "Not this cabin! My grandfather built it. He built all these buildings. Why would you tear them down?"

Mr. Wagner looks briefly in my direction then back at Dad and Aunt Laurel. "With your cooperation, I can transform this worthless wildland and these tacky little buildings into something truly remarkable. My architects will draw up a general plan," he says, "and my lawyers will write out an agreement. Both should be ready sometime next week. I'll make this project a top priority. Trust me, you won't regret your decision."

He shakes hands with Dad and Aunt Laurel. "Oh, and by the way," he says, "keep this to yourselves until everything is in place. Gossip runs rampant in backwaters like this and it can destroy even the most perfect plans."

He brushes past me, steps daintily into his truck and drives through the gate, leaving us to choke on his dust.

CHAPTER FOURTEEN

"YOU WON'T BELIEVE what Mountain Properties is planning," Aunt Laurel says, oozing enthusiasm and lit up like a flare. Every cell in my body snaps to attention. She leans forward, her fairy earrings dancing. "Honestly, it's unbelievable. They've made us a fabulously generous offer and we don't have to fix up a thing. They'll level this silly cabin and that messy garden." She pauses before practically crowing, "And build a five-star guest lodge with, get this, a golf course and..."

The cabin, the garden – flattened? "But Gramps built this cabin with his own hands. And he loved that garden. How can you let that man wipe it all out? And what about me? What about what I want?"

My questions bounce like bullets off Superman's chest. Aunt Laurel simply rolls on, her grin wide enough to split her lips. "As part of the deal, they'll let us spend two weeks a year at the lodge, free. Imagine that! And Mr. Wagner even talked about building a ritzy private party house at that very beach where we had our picnic yesterday."

"Think of it, Son," Dad says. "At least two weeks here. Every year. Free! We can sell this place *and* keep our connection to Canoe Lake. How good is that?"

Their faces beam like headlights.

"This place is mine. Shouldn't I have some say in what happens to it?"

The headlights dim.

"Mr. Wagner's a big-time developer," Dad says, "and this isn't just any old development he's planning. He wants to turn this place into a first-class green resort with an energy-efficient lodge, an all-natural golf course..."

"A what?"

"Trust me, Son. This is exactly what we need."

"A golf course? We need a golf course?"

"No, I'm talking about the whole package. This is the fresh start you talked about. Our chance for a new life, free from all the shadows of the past."

"That's what Mom and Gramps are to you, shadows?" I ask.

"Of course not," Dad says. "I love them as much as you do and we'll never, never forget them. But being here with everything the way it was reminds me too much of everything we've lost. It's too sad."

"Don't you see, Ari?" Aunt Laurel says. "This is my fresh start, too. With my share from the sale plus what Father left me, I can set up my own hair salon, exactly the way I want it. It's a dream come true."

"But you're throwing away Gramps' work, his whole life."

"We're not throwing anything away," Aunt Laurel says. "We're selling."

"Can't we just be happy, Ari? For once?" Dad says.

Outside, a bird sings. Branches sway. Clouds skim across the sky. Soon bulldozers will roar in. Bricks and glass will shoot up in place of trees. Parking lot pavement will smother the land. This quiet place will change forever. The cabin, the garden and the peaceful bay will become distant memories.

Is that really what Dad and Aunt Laurel want?

"Grab your jackets," Aunt Laurel says, "and let's go to town. We can buy some celebration supplies and treat ourselves to a first-class lunch at the finest restaurant we can find."

"No, thanks," I say.

Aunt Laurel rolls her eyes. "Suit yourself," she says, "but this deal is as good as done. Get used to it."

"I don't have to get used to it. I'm outta here. Get used to that."

Down the steps I go, across the yard, past Aunt Laurel's fancy steel gate, away from her, away from Dad, away from their crazy plans.

My shadow darts ahead of me, an enormous giant leading the way. If I were as big as my shadow, no one would ignore me or boss me around. No one would dare.

I'll run till my feet blister and bleed, till my lungs burst. I lift my arms over my head, higher, higher. A bird, spreading my wings. Ari Martin, ready for take-off.

As I speed down the road, my head begins to clear. I have no jacket, no food, no money, no...

Tires grind on gravel!

I dive into the thick brush at the side of the road and hunker down. An engine growls closer. My heart thumps. A vehicle roars by, spitting gravel, invisible through the branches. Are Dad and Aunt Laurel looking for me? Or are they busy planning their little celebration without me?

A mosquito buzzes in my ear. Another lands on my arm. I wave them away.

I let the dust and silence settle, then get up slowly and stretch my cramped muscles. I have to pee. But where? No bathroom, no public toilet, nothing but trees and bushes.

"Yeah, dummy," I shout out loud. "Nothing but trees and

bushes." I unzip my fly. Here, *Mr. Wagner. Develop this!* I spin a circle like a sprinkler. A flat rock catches my eye. A – R – I, I spell out wetly.

I'm Ari Martin, and this is my territory.

The last drop falls. I zip up and head for the road. Hey, a morel! At least now I won't starve. Do they taste good raw, or are they poisonous until you cook them? Are there more? More morels? I pick the mushroom carefully then search this way and that. No more morels. I slip my one mushroom into my pocket, wishing I had my backpack.

I walk back to where I started, if this is where I started. A – R – I has disappeared, dried up, and flat rocks are scattered everywhere. Where's the road? I walk left, no road. Right, still no road. Forward. Backward. This way? That way? Maybe another car will come. But when? This isn't exactly Lake Shore Boulevard.

A gust of wind chills my bare arms. I lean against a tree, shivering, fear tight in my throat.

A bird chirps. A squirrel chatters. My heart thuds. But the road is gone.

Tears prick my eyes.

Trees tower over me. A rotting log lies at my feet. My shadow, lost among a thousand others, can't guide me. Eventually all these shadows will melt together and join into night. I'll be alone in the dark. Lost.

I sit down, surrounded by rocks and leafy plants. The forest feels cool, indifferent. I could die here, reduced to food and fertilizer.

A line of ants troops by. I follow them with my eyes. Their line curves around a crushed flower. I get up, watching closer. A footprint, an overturned rock.

I can mark a trail, like I did at the creek. I'll move in widening circles, breaking branches, stacking rocks, whatever it takes to see where I've been until I reach the road.

Thick brush forces me to zigzag, but I mark the best circle I can.

Breathe in. Breathe out. Walk. Walk and mark trail. No thinking allowed.

I weave a path over rocks, around bushes, between trees. Branches scratch, slap and poke. Mosquitoes buzz and bite. Sweat prickles my skin.

The tangle thins, then I see it, like a ribbon dropped from the sky. The road!

CHAPTER FIFTEEN

I CAN'T GO BACK TO THE CABIN, not yet, even if Dad and Aunt Laurel aren't there, and especially if they are. What to do? Walk. Walk and think.

Would Gramps want a fancy resort? A golf course? Snooty strangers with pinched-up noses coming and going day after day, year after year?

Kids at school would turn purple knowing I had my own personal resort to go to every summer. They'd crowd around to hear my exciting stories about fishing trips and parties at the beach. I'd post pictures and videos everywhere.

But here in Canoe Lake I'd be an outsider, another guest with a faraway life and faraway friends, friends more interested in what I have than who I am.

Farm Fresh Eggs 4 Sale. That sign jolts me out of my thoughts and back onto the road. I never noticed that sign before.

"Hey, jogger boy, look up."

"Tam?"

"Up here." She grins down at me like a Cheshire cat perched on a high branch. "See what you miss if you don't look up? Whole universes go by, and you don't even notice. Come on up."

"Why don't you grab a vine and swing down?"

She slides down the tree like water. "In case you're wondering, I wasn't sitting in this tree waiting to ambush you. You were walking down the road in some sort of trance, and I thought from up there I could either snap you out of your daze or let you pass by, depending on whether I felt like talking to you or not."

"About what I said at the beach, I'm sorry..."

"Me too. I overreacted. What I said about no one owning the beach might be true in a perfect world, but in this world the Road Hag had every right to put up that gate and lock it. I just thought that now the land belongs to you, everything would change."

"I thought so too."

"Can't you just unlock the gate and tell your aunt to go fly a kite?"

"Sure. I'll open the gate if you'll give her the kite."

Tam cringes.

"The beach is only part of the problem. All my land could be scooped up by a..."

"Hey, Tam!" a voice calls from the Farm Fresh Eggs 4-Sale driveway.

"Hey, Justin," Tam calls back. "Look who's here."

Justin walks toward us, carrying a basket. When he sees me, he says, "Hey, neighbour. Have you had your breakfast, lunch, or brunch yet?"

"None of the above," I say, and my empty belly growls.

He holds out the basket filled with eggs. "Our hens were exceptionally generous this morning. And I'll bet you never tasted eggs like these, still warm from the hen."

"Gross."

"So you say now, Ari Martin, but sliver my almonds if these won't be the best eggs you ever tasted. My eggs Bennie are world-famous in Canoe Lake."

"Thursday mornings he practices his culinary skills," Tam says. "Chef Boy-our-Justin, we call him."

"Mom and Dad leave for a mere few hours to check the cattle on the range, and what happens?" Justin says. "Voilá, they create a cooking monster."

"Can you use this?" I ask, pulling the squashed morel out of my pocket.

"You bet. Morels go with everything." He drops the mushroom into his basket.

We walk down his driveway, flanking a pen busy with chickens. The birds, seemingly unaffected by the loss of their eggy offspring, cluck and peck, ignoring us completely. Only the rooster struts along beside us.

Eggs Benedict à la Justin comes with all the extra bacon I can eat, fresh fruit, crispy potatoes and trout with slices of hot, buttery morel. I all but lick the pattern off my plate.

"Did you catch this trout?" I ask Justin.

"Sure did," he says, "at Walter's secret hole. Have you been there yet?"

"Never, but how can it be secret if you know about it?"

"Some secrets are meant to be shared," Tam says. "That's what..."

"Gramps always said," I finish for her.

"It's supposed to rain later on," Justin says, "but if you want to see where it is, we can go right now."

CHAPTER SIXTEEN

JUSTIN'S PATH LEADS INTO THE FOREST, but unlike my trails, his is wide and well worn. We move quickly.

After several minutes, the rush of falling water grows into a roar. Tiny rainbows flicker through the trees. The trail ends.

Tam points. "The fishing hole's right below the waterfall."

"With a nice sandy beach and a rock bridge farther downstream," Justin says. "Best fishing and swimming hole ever!"

He leads the way down a narrow, slippery path. It switchbacks down more gently than my butt-slide on the other side of the creek. Still, my feet slip on the mud, sending pebbles and sticks rolling down the steep slope.

We stop at the end of the beach nearest the waterfall. Tam and Justin start skipping stones, but I sprawl out on the sand with my fingers laced under my head. I close my eyes and let the rumble of the waterfall flow through me.

I could get used to this.

"Look at those clouds," Tam says.

Black clouds plow across the sky, swallowing the last bits of blue. The wind picks up and a cold drop of rain splashes on my head.

BBSSSHHHHHUUUU! Lightning strikes a tall tree on the hillside we just came down, turning it into a giant torch.

Every hair on Tam's head flies out in a different direction.

I barely take a breath when CRASH! The loudest thunder I've ever heard rattles every cell in my body. Rain peppers the creek.

We huddle together under a small overhang and watch the rain, the waterfall, the creek. Lightning and thunder. The rain slows a bit, and Justin says, "Let's get out of here. This could go on for hours."

"But we can't go back the way we came, not by that burning tree," Tam says, her eyes wide.

"Me and my dad made a trail from our cabin to the other side of the creek," I blurt out, "looking for this fishing hole. It's a ways downstream."

"Let's go," Tam says.

We run for the rock bridge, pelted by rain.

Up close, the line of rocks looks more like a tightrope than a bridge. Tam and Justin cross as easily as if they're riding an escalator or strolling on a sidewalk.

"Ari?" Tam calls.

I step onto the first rock. My foot slips slightly and I have to pull it back. Water races by, dizzying and hypnotic. Rain pours from the sky. I put my arms out for balance and step again, teetering. Slowly, slowly. One step, then another. Step, balance. Step, balance. Slip, teeter, teeter, uh, oh, ah, balance. Step.

Almost there. I focus my eyes on the creek bank, bend my knees to push off from the last rock.

BANG! A clap of thunder throws off my timing and sends me flying. I land flat on my face in the gravelly sand with half of me still in the creek.

Tam and Justin pull me up from both sides. I shake sand from my hair and spit it out of my mouth. Shivering, I turn and splash cold creek water on my arms to wash off the blood.

"Are you okay, Ari?" Tam asks. "Can you walk?"

"I'd offer you my jacket," Justin says, "but it's soaked."

"I'm fine. Let's get moving." I start slogging downstream.

Lightning flashes. Rain tumbles in sheets. "How far?" Tam asks.

Good question.

CHAPTER SEVENTEEN

"Not much farther," I say as I hobble through the shallows on numb feet, searching for the spot where Dad and I came down to the creek.

"What should we be looking for?" Tam asks. "What colour ribbon did you mark your trail with?"

"Ribbon?"

"You know, that plastic flagging tape that comes in rolls," Justin says. "Walter always used red, but it also comes in blue, yellow, pink."

So that's what that box of ribbon was in Gramps' shed. "No ribbons," I say, "just a fairly steep slide and then a wide line of broken branches."

Slippery rocks and fast water threaten to knock my feet out from under me. A huge fallen evergreen blocks our path, forcing us to scramble through its prickly branches like spiders.

Where is that trail? Did I pass it? A logjam the size of an office building forces us up the hillside.

As I climb higher, the creek disappears behind a heavy green curtain. Its burble grows fainter and fainter until the rain drowns it out completely. I stop, hold my breath, listen.

"Dad and I never saw a logjam, so we must have to go

farther downstream," I say.

"I have a pretty good sense of direction," Justin says, "and I've been here longer than anyone. Why don't you follow me for a while?"

Part of me hates letting him lead, but a much bigger part is freezing cold, soaked to the bone and aching to get out of the rain.

Justin weaves through the bush. A single thread through the eyes of a hundred needles. My shoes and socks squish with every step. Cold rain trickles down my back. We edge our way back down to the creek.

And then I see our worm bucket!

"Over here!" I shout. "Follow me."

I pick up the bucket and head downstream to the spot where Dad's and my trail headed back to the cabin. We scramble up the hill and through the bush.

"When this dries out, I'll help you clear a better trail," Justin says.

"And I'll help you ribbon it," Tam says, "so next time you won't need a bucket to find it from the creek."

A glimpse of red over purple, blue, orange...Gramps' rainbow cabin!

And I, Ari Martin, lead my friends home.

At the edge of the garden, they stop. "Come on," I say. "Let's go inside and dry off. Aunt Laurel can drive you home after."

"Not quite ready for that," Tam says, through chattering teeth and blue lips.

"I'm pretty warm myself," Justin says, "and the rain seems to be letting up."

A second later, they're gone.

I head for the cabin, expecting a whole different kind of storm.

Before I reach the porch, Dad and Aunt Laurel run outside, both talking at once.

"Where were you?" Aunt Laurel asks. "You were gone all day. We were beside ourselves with worry waiting for you to come home."

"You're soaked and covered in mud," Dad says. "And is that blood on your arm?"

"Run the shower as hot as you can stand it," Aunt Laurel says as soon as we're inside.

"I'll put dry clothes in the bathroom for you," Dad says.

After a long thaw in the shower, I pull on the pajamas and robe Dad left on the toilet seat. When I open the door, steam pours from the bathroom and swirls around spicy pizza smells coming from the oven.

I expect the Spanish Inquisition, but all I get is a careful inspection of my scrapes and scratches. Dad dabs ointment on each one, gently.

"How did you get these?" he asks.

"Exploring the creek," I answer, leaving out my friends for now. "I think I found Gramps' fishing hole. It's as spectacular as you remembered."

"Was there a waterfall?"

I nod.

"A rock bridge and a little beach?"

"Sounds like the place," I say.

Aunt Laurel finishes tossing her salad and puts it on the table. She lifts a bubbling pizza out of the oven. "One side is vegetarian and the other has pepperoni for you and your dad."

Have I dropped into a parallel universe?

As we dig into our pizza, I say, "Finding Gramps' secret fishing hole got me thinking that I don't know where he is."

"What?" Dad and Aunt Laurel ask in unison, putting

down their pizza to stare.

"Gramps, where is he?"

"Ari!" Aunt Laurel snaps.

"You mean his spirit?" Dad asks. "Like in heaven?"

"No, I mean Gramps' grave isn't with Mom's in Toronto. Where is he buried?"

"He isn't," Dad says. "He's under my bed."

Aunt Laurel's face turns the colour of pond scum. "Must we talk about this now? It's hardly table conversation."

"He wanted to be cremated, and he wants us to scatter his ashes in the bay," Dad says softly.

Gramps? Ashes?

Aunt Laurel picks up her plate and stomps over to the sink. She drops it in with a loud clatter then marches into her room and slams the door.

Dad and I sit in frozen silence, our pizza cooling on our plates.

I have him all to myself. We can talk. But he chooses to tune his guitar instead.

Plunk, Plenk, Plink. Note by note, string by string, he concentrates on tuning. Each *plunk* brings me closer to grabbing the instrument and splintering it over his head.

"Dad, could you stop for a minute and listen? You know how Gramps wanted us to try living here?"

Plunk, twaaang. "And here we are."

"He meant living here, not just visiting."

Plunk, twaang.

"Well, I like it here. I'm actually making friends." Two statements I haven't uttered since Mom died.

Plunk, twang. "That's great, Ari. Really."

Plenk, twaaang.

"Remember what Gramps said in his letter about magic and adventure, about healing and putting down roots?"

Plenk, twaang.

"That's starting to happen, and in just a short time. If we stay, we might be happy again like we were with Mom. Even Aunt Laurel might chill out. We'd be a family."

Plenk, twang. Plink, plink, twaaang.

Finally, Dad says, "Stop, Ari, please. This place makes me too sad, and your aunt needs the money for her hair place. When Mr. Wagner brings the papers, we'll sign. Period. End of discussion. Goodnight."

He takes his guitar to his room and closes the door.

CHAPTER EIGHTEEN

AFTER A RESTLESS NIGHT, I wake up early, my mood as grey as the thin light shining through my window and skylight. Last night's raindrops thrum the roof with every puff of breeze. I go to the window and watch water from branches and leaves spill into puddles. The ground glistens.

Below me, Dad's soft strumming sounds almost like a song.

"Help yourself to some cereal," Aunt Laurel says as soon as I come down the ladder. "Then we'll all go look inside that storage building. It's the only way to shut your father up and end his litany of 'Is this in there? Is that in there?' If he asks me one more question about that stupid building, I'll go flat-out bonkers."

Dad continues to strum while I hurry to finish my cereal, trying not to imagine how Aunt Laurel could be any crazier.

Steam rises from the ground outside. The rain has stopped, but nothing is dry.

Dad heads for the car.

"Forget the car," Aunt Laurel says. "We have to walk. I'm not driving through any more long grass." She leads the way, but slowly, as if trying to stay dry on the wet path. "Father spent years collecting stuff," she says as we follow her through the grass on the far side of the cabin. "Everything I didn't throw out, I put in that building for safekeeping." She flashes a key dangling from a chain around her neck.

The path ends at a large building wrapped in white plastic. A shred of the plastic flaps in the breeze. Two doors face the trail: one wide enough for a vehicle, the other an ordinary outside door. Both are locked, and the plywood nailed over the windows prevents even a peek inside.

Aunt Laurel opens the smaller door and Dad's jaw nearly falls off his face. "Pop's truck! I knew he had a truck." He steps inside and runs his hand along the box of the cherry-red Chevy pickup packed full of treasures transplanted from the house.

"And his canoe!" He points to a red boat hanging from the rafters. "Pop sure loved red. And look," he practically crows, skipping across the room, "his fly-tying bench with all his fishing tackle and his good fly rods." He turns to me and Aunt Laurel. "Look at those tools behind you! A DeWalt table saw *and* a band saw, a wood lathe, a planer, top-of-the-line hand tools. And a complete set of woodcarving knives. Finishing that canoe I've been carving will be infinitely easier and more polished now."

"So that chunk of wood you've been mutilating is a canoe?" Aunt Laurel says.

Dad ignores her and continues caressing tools. "Pop told me he had tools, but I never imagined such a wide range or anything near this quality."

Something catches my eye at the back of the building. A bright red mountain bike! "Hey, look what I found!"

Dad walks over to me. "That was mine," he says. "Pop must have fixed it up for you."

"I can have it?"

"I'm sure that was the plan," Dad says.

Manoeuvering my new bike around a stack of boxes, I notice a door. "Hey, Aunt Laurel," I shout, "what's in here? The door is locked."

"Probably just more junk, but none of my keys fit. I've tried."

"I might know where the key is," I say. "I'll be right back."

I return in record time with the key from the garden shed. Dad and Aunt Laurel huddle around me as I slip it into the lock and swing the door open.

Aunt Laurel lets loose a string of loud hiccuping noises. At first I think she's laughing. But she bursts into tears.

Laughing would be a more sensible reaction to a room full of fairies.

Wooden fairies hang from the ceiling and cover every surface! Some have pointy, turned-up shoes. Others are barefoot and bare-headed. One has a raspberry cap; another sports a jaunty pine cone. Several dine around a mushroom table. More dance around a painted campfire, playing flutes and tambourines, laughing and singing to magical, invisible music.

"They're beautiful," Dad says, "stunning. Look at the detail. Hey, this one moves its wings! I had no idea Pop was such an artist."

Aunt Laurel blows her nose. A fairy trumpet? "Father did this for me, for me," she sobs. "He said he had a surprise for me if I came up, but I never imagined, never. How could I?"

"Better yet, how could *he*?" Dad says. "These must have taken years to make. But why fairies? I don't get it."

Aunt Laurel cups a daffodil fairy in her hands as if expecting it to fly away. "You wouldn't remember, James," she says. "You were too busy being a teenager. But our first summer here, the only one for me, all Mother wanted to do after she got stung by those wasps was go back to civilization."

"I remember that," he says. "To her dying day, she shuddered at the mere mention of this place."

"Exactly. Her mind was made up, so Father worked on me."

"You? How?" I ask.

"With fairies. He called me his fairy princess. Don't laugh. I was only ten and I loved it. Father put in a garden and I spent all summer helping him. He told me if we planted the seeds and cared for them, the fairies would help our plants grow. I spent hours weeding and watering, watering and weeding, but I never saw a single fairy."

Aunt Laurel weeding? Watering? Watching for fairies? Aunt Laurel?

"Every day I searched the berry patch, the pea vines, the wildflowers, certain that every fleeting shadow was a fairy. Father showed me a fairy ring in the forest as proof they lived nearby. Come autumn, I checked under potato plants and squash leaves. When winter came he told me snowflakes were fallen fairy wings, as if fairies molted like chickens. In the spring, he promised that when the last snow melted, the fairies would come out to celebrate. But before spring came, we moved to Vancouver. And that was the end of it. Time passed and I lost my interest in fairies."

Tears splash down her cheeks.

"So why the fairy earrings?" I ask.

"There was something about those days," she begins slowly, thinking. "Those days of searching the garden and the forest for fairies, those were the happiest days of my life. And now, every morning, for the tiniest instant when I put on my earrings, I catch a glimpse of that magic."

"Well, Aunt Laurel, you're in luck. Now you can stay here with enough fairies to keep you happy all day long."

When she locks up the building, each of us takes a bit of

treasure back to the cabin: I walk my bike, Dad packs his box of woodcarving knives and Aunt Laurel coddles her daffodil fairy as if a puff of wind might blow it away.

When we get to the cabin the phone is ringing.

CHAPTER NINETEEN

AFTER ANOTHER RESTLESS NIGHT and a lot of swearing, I'm headed for our gate on my new red bike. Dad and Aunt Laurel are on their way to town to buy supplies for their so-called Big Sale Celebration. Before they left, I had to swear I'd be super-duper careful on my bike. "Look and look again before you turn or cross an intersection. Ride on the shoulder, not in the middle of the road. Don't pedal too fast. Don't take any risks or dangerous trails."

I made Dad and Aunt Laurel swear and double swear on everything that matters to them that they wouldn't go to town and sell my place behind my back.

All this swearing began yesterday after Mr. Wagner called to say "his people" had drawn up the necessary paperwork, including a resort sketch, and he'd bring everything to the cabin first thing Monday morning for Dad and Aunt Laurel to sign.

When I objected, Dad said, "Forget it, Ari, we can't pass up this offer."

And things went downhill from there.

Now here I am, trusting them not to sell my place out from under me. And they're trusting me not to die on my bike.

I turn left at the end of my driveway and head for Tam's.

This would be the best ride ever, if I could think of a way to stop Mr. Wagner or at least stall him. Last night I fell asleep counting gross ingredients I could combine into a disgusting mixture to pour on those oh-so-important papers. Ketchup? No. Not gross enough. Mustard? Maybe. Tofu and cow poo? Definitely.

Better yet, I'd get rid of those stinking papers once and for all. Send them to the bottom of the lake. Or throw them in a campfire and roast marshmallows over them. But what if he has copies?

Mr. Foster gave me his business card and told me to call if I had any questions or concerns. I have plenty of both, and he might know a better way to slow down Mr. Wagner and Mountain Properties' big takeover of my land. Lawyers know stuff like that.

Tam's gate! Already. This bike moves fast.

The cows are nibbling grass at the far end of the field, so my bike and I get through the gate and to her door without a hitch.

"Ari," Tam says. "What brings you here?"

"Can I come in?"

She opens the door wide. Remembering I'm back in Japan, I kick off my shoes.

"I have the place to myself today," she says as I follow her into the kitchen. "Except for the kittens, of course. Your little runt is growing. Come see."

My kitten is rolling around in the box with one of her siblings. She's even cuter than I remember. Her shiny black coat and white feet flash a memory of Mom's white shoes that she called her sneakers.

"Good little Sneakers," I say, stroking her silky fur.

"Sneakers, eh?" Tam says. "I like that name, and Miss

Marmalade seems to approve."

We sit on the floor and watch Miss Marmalade lick her kittens while they play.

"You're not just stopping by to check on your kitten, are you?" Tam says.

"Have you ever heard of Mountain Properties or J.P. Wagner?" I ask.

She shakes her head no.

"According to the logo on his truck, Mr. Wagner is the president of Mountain Properties. He wants to buy my property and tear down everything Gramps built to put in a lah-dee-dah resort with a lodge, a golf course and a private party house at the beach. He's bringing the papers Monday for Dad and Aunt Laurel to sign. They'd rather have the money than the land, so they'll sign, and I don't think I can stop them."

"Hold on a second," Tam says. "They can sell your property without your permission?"

I nod, fighting tears. "They haven't even given Canoe Lake a chance. It's the first place I've ever felt I could truly belong. I want to learn everything about it: what grows here, who lives here, everything. But on Monday my chance to do that could disappear forever." I have to stop to breathe.

"You're not giving up without a fight," Tam says. "You must have a plan."

"It's happening too fast. One day I inherit Gramps' land, and the next day Mr. Wagner comes along and wants to buy it."

"Do you know anything about him?" she says.

"Nothing."

"So let's find out who we're dealing with."

Despite having no cell service, Tam's house isn't as electronically challenged as Gramps'. I follow her to a small office, where we search the Web for Mr. Wagner (no J.P.) and Mountain Properties (fancy website, no hard data).

"That's odd," she says.

"I know someone who might be able to help us. Gramps' *lawyer*." The word sounds strange coming out of my mouth. "My lawyer. I have his card."

"Call him," Tam says, handing me a cordless phone. "We need all the help we can get."

"Thank you for calling Sanders and Foster. Our office is closed today, but please leave a message and we'll get back to you as soon as possible."

Trying not to sound whiny, I ask if Mr. Foster can help keep Mr. Wagner and Mountain Properties from buying my land on Monday.

Will he get my message in time? Will he even remember a dorky kid he's only seen once?

"Why not email him too?" she says. "He might answer emails even when he's not at his office."

I send my email.

"Anything else we can do?" Tam asks.

"When Mr. Wagner comes, we could flatten his tires, grab the sale papers and run," I suggest.

"Or we could stand hand in hand in the middle of the road and not let him pass."

"We could smear cow pies on the papers."

"Or we could round up Justin's cattle and chase him off with a stampede," she says.

We go back and forth with mostly bad ideas until one idea hits me so hard I nearly fall over.

"I've got it! I've got it!" I tell Tam. "It's simple but perfect. And so obvious. How could I have missed it?"

Tam and I go over every detail. I'm risking everything on a single plan. It has to work.

CHAPTER TWENTY

DAD AND AUNT LAUREL are already home when I get there. Dad's sitting on the porch, whittling. "Quick trip," I say.

"Not much to do in a town like Moose Valley," he says. "How's the new bike?"

"Great. Hey, your little canoe is looking good."

"Thanks. Pop's tools make a big difference."

"So all you did in town was buy supplies?"

"We didn't sell this place, if that's what you're asking," Dad says without looking up.

I go inside. Aunt Laurel is painting her nails at the table. A big bakery box sits across the table from her. I lift the lid and read the blue frosting letters. "Congratulations?"

"It was that or 'Happy Birthday'. Special orders take two days. We'll freeze the cake till Monday, then bring it out to celebrate the big sale. I even bought champagne," she says, dipping the tiny brush into the bottle of purple polish.

As much as I want my plan to work, my time here could be ending. I could lose, and if I do, I want to leave my own mark on this place, something that shows I was here. And happy to be here. Like Gramps. Even if bulldozers tear it all down.

I go to the garden shed and pull on a pair of work gloves,

pick up a hammer, a box of nails, a can of paint and a brush. I carry everything to the old swing and start pulling weeds.

Sweat pours down my face and drips down my back, but the hotter I get, the harder I pull until every weed around that swing is gone. Some of the wooden cross-pieces on the swing are wobbly. A board on the seat is loose. I pick up the hammer and a nail and start pounding. Wham. Wham. Wham.

I take another nail and pound some more. Wham. Wham. Wham. Again and again.

Tap. Tap. Tap.

What?

"Dad!" He's hammering his own nails into the side of the swing behind me.

"This cedar has certainly stood the test of time," he says. "Pop built things to last."

Tap. Tap. Tap. Wham. Wham. Wham. Tap. Tap. Tap. Together we fix up the swing until it's so strong a tornado couldn't knock it down.

"Now let's paint it," I say.

Dad picks up the can of red paint I brought and says, "I saw some weather-resistant stain in the shop. No sense covering up this beautiful wood."

"But red was Gramps' favourite colour. It fits in with his rainbow cabin," I say.

"Red it is then," Dad says. "I'll get another brush."

Even Aunt Laurel can't resist coming outside to watch me and Dad turn a rickety relic into a masterpiece. "What's the point of painting that old thing?" she says.

"Wait and see," Dad says.

"How long till we can try it?" I ask.

"It should be dry by tomorrow," Dad says, touching up a final spot with his brush and smiling.

And so it is. After breakfast Sunday morning, we all troop outside to admire the swing.

"Where's the camera?" Dad asks.

"I'll get my cell," Aunt Laurel says, "if I can remember where I left it."

By the time she returns, Dad and I are swinging away. She snaps a shot.

"Is that the first picture we've taken this whole time?" I ask.

"Could be," she says.

"Come sit between us, Sis," Dad says, "and we'll take a group shot."

Our first family photo since the accident, right back here on the swing. A shiver runs down my spine. Is something bad about to happen, like it did after our last family photo?

CHAPTER TWENTY-ONE

I WAKE UP MONDAY MORNING to the sound of high heels clicking on the floor: Aunt Laurel, ready for action. The epic wrestling match between Ari Martin and Mountain Properties is about to begin. Hold on to your hats, ladies and gents. This could get ugly.

I dress and climb down the ladder.

"Morning," I mumble. Dad nods and continues to butter his toast. Aunt Laurel pauses from checking out her lipstick in a small mirror and glances briefly in my direction. I reach into the cupboard for a cereal bowl.

Knock, knock, knock.

"Mr. Wagner? So early?" Aunt Laurel runs to the door.

Tam, Evan and Justin stand in the doorway, scrunched together like ducklings trying to look like one big duck.

"Who's there?" Dad asks, getting up.

"Who are you?" Aunt Laurel demands.

"They're my friends," I say. "Come in."

Tam's hair looks like it's on permanent lightning alert. The part in Justin's hair has more bends than the road into town. Evan's bangs zig and zag across his forehead.

Justin speaks first, "I'm Justin Owens, and this is Tam and her little brother Evan." They step cautiously into the cabin, kick off their shoes and slide them away from the door.

"You know Ari?" Dad asks.

"Yep, we're his friends and your new neighbours dropping by for a little visit," Justin says. "We brought you some smoked trout."

Dad takes the plate of fish. "You caught this?"

"Yep, and I used hickory wood to smoke it." Justin grins at me. "Next time we'll be firing up the smoker for Ari's catch."

"Why is your gate always locked?" Evan asks.

Aunt Laurel gasps. "Oh no! The gate! Run and open it, Ari. Hurry."

For once I do what she says, though not for the reason she thinks.

"I'll help," Tam says, shoving her feet into her shoes and following me out the door.

Aunt Laurel hovers in the doorway, her lips clenched, her chin jutting forward.

Tam and I run as fast as we can to the shed, grab the key and run for the gate. I unlock it, and Tam swings it open.

On our way back to the cabin, she asks the same question that's been racing through my head, "What if...our plan... doesn't work?" She huffs the words to the beat of our speeding feet. "What'll...we do...then?"

We burst into the cabin, panting.

"I'm James," Dad says to Tam, "and that's my sister, Laurel, over there. It's been a long time since I've met any of Ari's friends. Would you like something to drink? Hot chocolate? Juice?"

Tam, no longer the fearless warrior, cowers in the presence of the Road Hag. She stands stiff as a wooden soldier while Evan and Justin sit and drink juice at the table. "I, um, uh, I don't need anything to drink," she stammers. "Thanks anyway." She edges closer to me and adds in a whisper, "Do we have a Plan B?"

"What did you say?" Aunt Laurel swoops in like a vulture, looming over Tam, who has turned deathly pale.

Knock, knock, knock.

Dad opens the door and ushers in an older woman with bright green hair carrying a small dog in her arms. "Remember us?" Millie asks, letting Peppy loose on the floor so she can hold up her basket. "Today I brought a nice cinnamon apple loaf and more of Bertie's butter." She puts the food on the table and turns to Aunt Laurel. "I tried putting them streaks in my hair like yours, but it didn't quite work. You think you could fix it?"

Dad and Aunt Laurel exchange glances, but before they can say or do anything, we hear another knock. I put on the kettle.

Justin and Evan put their glasses in the sink. "Let the show begin," Justin whispers, flashing me a grin. He and Evan steer Tam over to the couch for front-row seats.

"What's going on here?" Aunt Laurel asks on her way to the door. Fairies tremble in her earlobes. This time, a whole family waits outside.

"Good morning," the man says. "We're the Washburns."

"Yes, I'm sure you are," Aunt Laurel says. "The question is, what are you doing here?"

"We just stopped by for a little visit, m'am," the man says. "Well, look here, if it isn't Millie Marshall. 'Morning, Millie."

"'Morning, Henry, Eileen. And how are Maddi and Mikey this morning?"

The two little ones hide behind their parents.

"Could someone please tell me what's going on?" Aunt Laurel sounds frightened.

"It isn't often we have guests," Dad says, trying to smooth

things over.

"Guests are generally invited, James," Aunt Laurel corrects.

"Sorry if we caught you at a bad time," Eileen says. "We just felt it was high time we let you know how sorry we are about Walter's passing and at the same time how pleased we are to have his family here."

Aunt Laurel mumbles something in response.

"Thought you might like to try our homemade goat cheese," Eileen says, pulling two neatly wrapped packages out of her bulging purse and placing them on the table.

Aunt Laurel eyes the gifts and her guests like biology specimens. Eileen's hair hangs in tangles, Maddi's pigtails are crooked and Mikey's hair is plastered to his head, just like his dad's.

"Millie tells me you cut hair," Eileen says. "Would you be interested in trading haircuts for manicures or pedicures?" She flashes ten perfectly painted fingernails. "I never mastered hair, but before we moved up here, I did a lot of nails."

"Looks like you still do," Aunt Laurel says, clasping her hands to hide her own nails.

The kettle whistles. I turn off the burner and prepare a teapot.

Another knock.

This time, Ben stands in the doorway with a platter of pastries. Both his hair and his beard are badly hacked. "Good morning," he says. "I'm Ben, Walter's partner in crime, and these are Walter's and my secret recipe, raspberry-filled doughnuts. Wait till you taste 'em. They'll melt in your mouth."

Ben introduces Justin's parents, Willow and Zack, who follow him inside. Willow's hair is spiked with barrettes. Zack seems to have started a bird's nest hotel on his head.

"So this is Ari, our newest property owner," Zack says. "Pleased to meet Walter's grandson and heir."

"H-how do you know about Ari's inheritance?" Aunt Laurel sputters like water in hot grease.

"News travels fast around here," Zack explains, "especially good news."

"But – but what do you want from us?" Aunt Laurel looks genuinely confused.

"We want you to feel at home and know you have people here who can help if you ever need anything," Willow says, offering two cartons of fresh farm eggs to Aunt Laurel, who makes no move to take them. Willow sets them on the counter.

I take out cups and plates. Ben, Zack and Henry sit at the table with Dad. Aunt Laurel, silent and pale, stands off to the side, ringed by guests.

More people come to the door, people I've never seen. People with hair in dire need of professional attention.

The name Walter floats freely around the cabin, almost as if he were here. For the first time since Gramps died, thinking of him makes me smile. *He is here with his family and friends, all of us, together.*

Countless conversations join the clinking of cups and forks. Maddi and Mikey run back and forth playing a giggling game of tag, their shyness forgotten. Peppy darts after them, yipping and wagging his tail.

Aunt Laurel backs over to Dad and yanks his sleeve until he gets up. She leads him to the corner by the sink. I slide in beside them, listening.

"What'll we do?" she says. "We can't sign papers in a mob like this."

A smile spreads across my face.

But then Dad says, "No one chases people off better than

you, Sis. Go on, get 'em!"

Aunt Laurel's voice thunders over the commotion filling the room. "Attention, everyone! Quiet! Please!"

A few people look up – briefly – before returning to their conversations.

Aunt Laurel ups her volume. "Listen! All of you have to leave. We're expecting an important visitor."

"And what are we, peanut butter?" Ben asks, grinning. A few people chuckle, but no one moves. The chat-fest resumes.

Aunt Laurel draws a long breath, no doubt preparing to shout something like "Get out of here. Now!" when Dad takes her arm.

"Let them be," he says. "We can wait for Mr. Wagner outside. When he gets here, we'll go over to the shop and sign the papers there." He leads his sister to the door. "Make yourselves at home everyone," he calls over his shoulder.

Tam, Evan and Justin leap up from the couch and weave their way over to me.

We step onto the porch in time to catch a flash of silver pulling through the gate. Aunt Laurel sprints over to it, faster than I've ever seen her move. Her high heels fly off her feet, but she doesn't stop. I run after her, my sock-footed friends right behind me. Dad brings up the rear.

The truck spins around, shooting up a rooster tail of dust. Aunt Laurel grabs the door handle before the truck has completely stopped. Mr. Wagner lowers the window.

"Did you bring the papers?" she puffs.

CHAPTER TWENTY-TWO

"WHY ARE ALL THESE VEHICLES IN YOUR YARD?" Mr. Wagner asks.

"Oh, those." Aunt Laurel flicks her hand vaguely, dismissing them. "Just some neighbours, you know, stopping by. Nothing to worry about."

"Don't expect me to park clear out here and ruin my expensive shoes tramping through the dirt."

"No, of course not. We can sign the papers right here. And once the deal is done, I'll bring out cake and champagne to celebrate."

Mr. Wagner reaches for his briefcase.

I push myself over to the window. "Hold on. No one's signing anything."

Aunt Laurel pushes me away, reclaiming the window. "Ari means *he* doesn't have to sign anything, just me and you and James."

Mr. Wagner takes out a stack of papers and a pen. Aunt Laurel reaches for them.

"I mean no one's signing anything." My three friends and I squeeze in front of her. Dad moves in behind us.

We look like a choir about to serenade a truck.

Aunt Laurel tries to smile. "Kids," she says, shoving all of us aside. "Just give me the papers and we'll get this over with."

Curious guests start trickling out of the cabin.

Mr. Wagner raises the pen and papers again, but I push them away.

"No!" I shout. "This place is mine. Gramps gave it to me. And you're crazy if you think I'm going to stand here and let you sign it over to some fancy-dancy guy in a truck. Dad and Aunt Laurel, you haven't even read these papers. How do you know what you're signing?"

"Ari does have a point," Dad says. "We *should* read them before we sign them."

"Shut up, James," Aunt Laurel shrieks. "Don't listen to him, Mr. Wagner."

More guests pour out of the cabin. A giant wave rolling right at us.

"What's going on here?" Mr. Wagner says. "I don't know what you're trying to pull, but I didn't come here to be harassed by a kid and chased by a scruffy mob."

"Just hand over those papers, Mr. Wagner." Aunt Laurel's face is practically purple. "We'll sign them right here, right now, and that will be that."

"I should hope so," Mr. Wagner says. "Let's get this over with."

She reaches inside the truck for the papers, but I grab them and throw them back at Mr. Wagner.

"Nice grab, Ari," my friends cheer. "Way to go!"

Mr. Wagner rolls up his window, guns his engine and tears off down the road.

"What just happened?" Dad says. "Why the big push to sign those papers today? When he saw we had guests, couldn't he have left them for us to go over later and sign when things quieted down?"

"No papers, no sale!" Tam throws her arms around me and jumps up and down. "The place is yours, Ari! Yours!"

"Not if I can help it," Aunt Laurel says. "Wait here, James. I'll get the car."

"And go where?" Dad says. "Our yard is gridlocked."

"Listen up everybody. Move your vehicles. I need to leave. Now!" Aunt Laurel shouts. "This is an emergency. I repeat, *this is an emergency!*"

Still barefoot, she plows through her guests, into the cabin and back out, carrying shoes, car keys and her purse. "Quick, James, get in the car," she yells.

"I'm going too," I say.

Peppy runs between our legs, yipping, with Millie right behind him, yelling, "Peppy, Peppy, Peppy!"

Millie scoops Peppy into her arms then catches up with Aunt Laurel just as she's opening the car door. With a talon-like grip, she grasps Aunt Laurel's shoulder, turns her around and speaks to her, nose to nose. "I got something to tell you that you need to hear, and I'll put it in terms you'll be sure to understand. Canoe Lake is like hair. It grows on you. Us neighbours'll grow on you too. Wait and see. We're not half bad once you get to know us."

"Neither am I." Aunt Laurel twists away from Millie and climbs into the driver's seat. She steps into her shoes and revs the engine, forcing Millie to run for the safety of the porch.

Cars and trucks back up and pull forward, moving in every direction at once, like a giant anthill struck by a boot.

As soon as a path clears, we whoosh off, tires squealing.

"Slow down, Laurel," Dad yells. "You're not the race car driver you think you are."

Shoulders hunched over the wheel, she slams her foot back and forth between the accelerator and the brake. Scenery blurs by.

I rocket from side to side, back and forth, up and down, bashing my head, butt, arms, legs, knees. No body part escapes un-bumped. My seat belt prevents my launch into space. But not so the contents of my stomach. A milky four-doughnut/smoked-trout mixture flies out the window, streaking out behind us like a comet's tail.

"Look! Up ahead. A truck! That must be him." Aunt Laurel floors the accelerator.

Speeding around curves, she catches up to a white, not silver, pickup with two teenagers inside. One has a pony tail, the other a ball cap. We whiz by them.

"Drat," she mutters. "From further back, I was sure that was him."

Dad, now as green as I am, shouts, "Slow down, Laurel. I mean it. You're gonna kill us."

A deer darts in front of us.

Aunt Laurel slams on the brakes, sending the car spinning.

CHAPTER TWENTY-THREE

THE RIGHT FRONT FENDER strikes the young buck, but he keeps running, into the bush and out of sight. The car comes to rest facing back the way we came.

"Pull onto the shoulder, Laurel. Now." Dad's using a voice I haven't heard for a long time. And Aunt Laurel listens.

Seconds tick by in silence.

He pulls the keys from the ignition. "I'll check the fender," he says, opening his door, "and I'm taking these so you won't go racing off without me."

Aunt Laurel slumps over the steering wheel and starts sobbing. Whether for the deer or her lost opportunity, I can only guess.

I climb out of the car, grateful to stand on my own two feet again.

"We were so lucky, unbelievably lucky," Dad says, pulling a few coarse brown hairs from the hole where the headlight once was.

"What about the deer?" I ask. "Was he lucky, too?"

"I hope so...I think so. We didn't hit him hard. We barely nicked him."

"Can we go after him?"

"We'd never find him. We have no idea where he might

have gone, and deer can go a long way on adrenaline. The best we can do is report this. Besides, we have our own wild creature to tend."

When Dad opens her door, Aunt Laurel is still slumped over the steering wheel, sobbing. "I'll find someplace quiet where we can figure out what to do. Scoot over and I'll drive." He nudges her into the passenger seat and buckles her in. I climb in back.

Dad's driving is as slow and careful as Aunt Laurel's was fast and reckless. He turns down a side road and pulls into a wide, sunny spot.

"Come on, Sis. A few minutes outside will clear our heads."

She opens her door. "Eeeww," she says, scrunching up her face at the dust-covered puke on the side of the car.

Dad leads her to a patch of wildflowers and sits her down on his jacket.

"Oh, James," she sighs, "what will we do?"

Dad shrugs. "Haven't a clue. But if you have Mr. Wagner's card, we could drive into town and call him."

"Ari, would you bring my purse from the car...please?"

Has my aunt ever addressed me this meekly and politely? I dally as long as possible on my errand, in no hurry to find Mr. Wagner.

Aunt Laurel searches frantically through her purse. "I...I can't find his card. I can't remember ever getting it. Did you, James?"

"Come to think of it, no."

"I suppose that since he always came to see us and everything was happening so fast, we never thought to ask for a card. I guess we could look for him in town."

"And if we don't find him?" Dad says.

"This must be a sign from Gramps," I say, "trying to save us from selling too soon. He's giving us some time to think."

"I doubt that. Father..."

Tic-tic-tic-tic-tic-tic-tic. PLOP.

Aunt Laurel screams. I duck. Dad flings his body over me and his sister. "Don't move," he says. "I'll protect you."

Two squirrels scuttle by, chasing each other, chattering and scolding.

"Squirrels?" Dad's voice rises as they scamper up a tree trunk. "I'm protecting my family from squirrels?"

"Well, you gotta start somewhere. Why not with squirrels?"

Dad laughs. So do I. And finally, Aunt Laurel. Our laughs rise into giggles and cascade into hilarity. Tears slide down our cheeks.

"This...isn't...funny," Aunt Laurel splutters and laughs harder. Laughter shakes her whole body, ambushing her, seizing this moment to have its way with her, having been locked out for so many years.

Laughing harder, Dad says, "What would Pop say, seeing his progeny panicked by a skittering pair of squirrels?"

"Not to mention the ominous PLOP." Aunt Laurel laughs. "What was that anyway? A pine cone?"

"Or maybe just a nut," I gasp out between giggles. "I was much braver with the bear."

The laughter stops.

"Bear? What bear?" Aunt Laurel asks.

Oops. I look at Dad. He shakes his head.

"A small bear," I say, "sort of a teddy bear really, a bear with no interest in me."

"A bear?" she repeats. "A real bear?"

"No worries. He never noticed me."

Dad wraps his arms around me, the first hug he's given me in ages.

Aunt Laurel puts her arms around us too. A family hug.

"We have to look after each other," she says. "Few as we are, we're still a family."

I brush a fly from her shoulder. Flowers bob in the breeze.

Dad drives home. Slowly. Not one car waits in the yard. The gate is open, but the silver pickup hasn't returned.

"Close the gate behind us, Ari," Dad says.

"No, leave it open," Aunt Laurel says.

"You think Mr. Wagner might come back?" Dad asks.

"Maybe," she says, "maybe not, but let's leave it open, just in case."

Inside the cabin is spotless, eerie in its tidy silence. Aunt Laurel's high heels stand neatly by the door. Covered plates of treats line the kitchen table.

Dad flops onto the couch, puts up his feet and closes his eyes. Aunt Laurel heads for the bathroom. I go to the sink for a long drink.

With the water running, no one hears the vehicle pulling into our yard.

Knock, knock, knock.

Dad groans. "Now what?"

CHAPTER TWENTY-FOUR

Aunt Laurel flies out of the bathroom and runs to the door. "Mr. Wagner?" she says as she reaches for the knob.

"Miss Martin, I'm so glad I found you! I'm Darcy Foster, the lawyer, remember? I hope I'm not too late?"

"Late for what?" she asks.

"You haven't signed any papers, have you?"

Dad and I snap to attention. The three of us stand together and stare.

"After I got Ari's messages," Mr. Foster begins.

"What messages?" Dad and Aunt Laurel turn their attention from Mr. Foster to me.

"His phone message and email." Mr. Foster looks puzzled, but he continues. "Anyway, I checked out this Mr. Wagner and his Mountain Properties. Turns out he's a fraud."

"A fraud?" Aunt Laurel squeaks. "What do you mean?"

"I'll tell you what I know, but first and foremost, have you signed anything?" Mr. Foster asks.

"No, not yet," Aunt Laurel says.

"Mr. Wagner came by with the papers this morning," Dad says, "but he took off before we could do anything."

"Well, thank the sun, moon and stars for that. Had you signed those papers, you could have lost your entire inheritance."

Aunt Laurel and Dad gasp. "What? How?"

"Simply put, between Mr. Wagner and his crooked lawyer, you could have signed away this house, this land, everything you own. You could have spent years battling him in court until you had no money, either, leaving you with nothing."

"N-n-nothing?" Aunt Laurel stammers. "B-but why? Why us?" Dad's face is pale.

"Fraudsters like Mr. Wagner, if that's even his real name, prey on vulnerable families. Conning is their business, and they're good at it. According to the RCMP, this guy studies recent death certificates, researches the estate, then closes in with a custom-made con."

"What about Mountain Properties?" I ask.

"Mountain Properties is nothing but a website and a magnetic sign he attaches to his truck."

"Will he be back?" Dad asks.

"Hard to say," Mr. Foster says. "It's likely he'll figure this jig is up and move on to his next victim. If he does show up, phone the police immediately."

"What do we do now?" Aunt Laurel asks.

"That's up to you," Mr. Foster says. "But if you still want to sell, be sure to take plenty of time to check out the offer before you agree to anything. You might choose to sell some of the raw land and keep the land with the buildings. There are other options as well. It's your call."

Dad sighs. "I'm not ready to deal with all that again."

"So don't," I say firmly. "You have a great shop here, loaded with enough tools to build or remodel anything and a huge wood supply with all these trees. Think of the possibilities, Dad."

"I will," he says. "And there's something else. Ben offered to give me guitar lessons. He and Zack play in a band. They said we could jam together."

"But what about me?" Aunt Laurel whines. "What'll I do? What about my hair salon?"

"I could help you fix up a place," Dad says. "And if you need more cash, you could borrow from my share of our inheritance. It's not a lot, but if it would help..."

"You'd do that? For me?"

"Or you could stay with us and cut hair here." The words escape before I can stop them.

Aunt Laurel's eyes fill with tears. I'll bet her eyes haven't been this well watered in years. "I can't stay, Ari. I'm just too much of a city girl to live here full time."

"So come part time," Dad says.

"Yeah, Aunt Laurel. Have scissors, will travel."

"I guess I could schedule appointments for a few days every month. People in this community could clearly use my services. And I'd love to get Eileen's hands on my nails."

"Excuse me," Mr. Foster says. "You have family matters to settle and I should get going."

"How about a slice of cake first?" Dad says. "And champagne."

"Thanks, but I have some catching up to do back at my office."

With a flurry of handshakes, thank-yous and goodbyes, we send Mr. Foster back to his office.

"We have catching up of our own to do," Dad says, "but let's eat first. That cake is huge."

"I'll ride my bike to Tam's, and together we'll round up everyone and bring them back for cake, champagne, and a proper send-off for Gramps."

"Wait. How...?" Aunt Laurel begins.

But before she can finish, I'm out the door, feeling light enough to fly.

Acknowledgements

I'd like to thank my writing support team: Becky Citra, Ainslie Manson and Ann Walsh for cheerfully listening to and critiquing more versions of *Between Shadows* than anyone (but me) should ever have to. The Banff Writing with Style program helped get the story rolling. Grenfell Featherstone's early-on editorial guidance kept it from going off track. Thanks to him, no one gets chased by farm animals. Sheryl Salloum, Janet Ames and Maggie deVries offered encouragement when I needed it most. Kathy Stinson, editor extraordinaire, found the best in *Between Shadows* and helped make it shine. Sandy Foster freely shared his legal expertise along with his infinite patience and enthusiasm. Larry Ramey explained and demonstrated the finer points of fishing. Frank Urbschat gave critical real estate advice. Huge appreciation also goes to my husband Mark for never doubting my ability and to my wonderful family, friends and neighbours who get me away from my desk and into the real world. Finally, thank you to Nik Burton and his talented colleagues at Coteau Books for seeing this project's potential and giving me the opportunity to see it through.

About the Author

KATHLEEN COOK-WALDRON is the author of numerous books for younger and older children, including Canadian Children's Book Centre Choice *Five Stars for Emily* and Best Books for Kids and Teens picture book selection *Forestry A to Z*. Kathleen lives and writes in 100 Mile House, BC.